The Game Owes Me: Basketball, Brotherhood, and the Cost of Greatness

Martinis Jackson & Manny Geraldo II

Martinis Jackson and Manny Geraldo II Publishing Company

ISBN: 979-8-9999375-0-6

Edited by: O Marie Dosier

This is a work of fiction: Names, characters, businesses, places, events, and incidents are either the products of the author's imagination or are used in a fictitious manner. Any resemblance to actual persons, living or dead, or actual events is purely coincidental.

Printed in the United States of America.

Contents

Prologue

Last Summer

On the outskirts of Atlanta, inside a converted industrial warehouse, teams from all over the country crowded around to watch the final game of the Baller's Circuit—youth basketball's highest stage of summer competition. The warehouse featured four pristine hardwood courts, divided by rusty support beams and makeshift curtains. Portable aluminum stands hugged the sidelines for spectators. Big-name college coaches sat courtside on folding chairs, scouting their future stars.

At center court stood Stephon Johnson, a rising junior with "Memphis Mayhem" emblazoned across his jersey. His biceps were sculpted from endless push-ups and pull-ups, and his locs draped over lean shoulders like tiny ropes sprawled over bronze hills. He glanced at the scoreboard, which was tied with five seconds remaining. The starting point guard for NY City Elite sank the front end of a one-and-one. 77-76. NY City Elite now had the lead.

Stephon's eyes swept the bleachers until he found his father, seated beside his two sisters. Their eyes locked, sharing a silent understanding. Stephon knew exactly what was expected. A simple nod between them conveyed it all.

He scanned the sidelines again, absorbing the sight of dozens of college coaches scribbling notes: 35 points, 7 assists, 5 rebounds. It was already a statement game, but he had one more chance to make his mark.

Swish. NY Elite sank the second free throw. 78-76. A clingy defender blanketed Stephon at half court, with another lurking near the free-throw line, hoping to deny him the ball. From the stands, Stephon's father just smiled. He knew something NY Elite didn't.

On the baseline, Stephon's teammate slapped the ball. Stephon exploded with four hard strides toward it, drawing the spy defender up and baiting the man behind to crowd too close. Then, in a flash, he stopped on a dime and cut back — so sharply that he left both defenders stumbling. His eyes found the ball sailing over their heads toward half court. Stephon caught it in stride like a seasoned wide receiver.

Four seconds.

A defender lunged, swiping greedily at the ball in Stephon's right hand — but it vanished behind his back, sending the defender sprawling into the bleachers. A collective gasp rose from the crowd.

Two seconds.

Stephon rose up from the three-point line as a defender's arms flailed out, grasping for a life preserver. Too late. The ball was gone, already arcing toward destiny.

The buzzer sounded. The net snapped.

Stephon's father jumped up, pumping his fist and shouting above the roar. Stephon's teammates stormed the court, crashing into his chest and lifting him off the ground in a wild swirl of celebration.

Following the championship and MVP ceremony, the conversations with college coaches, and the goofy griddy dances with teammates, Stephon and his father, Camron, sat on the baseline, sharing their ritual postgame moment—the one Stephon cherished most.

"Mr. MVP!" Camron pulled his son in for a tight embrace. "What'd I tell you? Didn't I tell you we were gonna do it?" His grin stretched from ear to ear. Stephon tried to speak through the breath-stealing hug.

"Yessir." He laughed, smiling the way only a son could when he knew he'd made his father proud.

"You know that coach down in Florida was talking to me at halftime," Camron said, resting an arm around Stephon's shoulders as they strolled toward the exit. "He graduated four All-Americans just last year."

"Florida?" Stephon's brow wrinkled. "But what about the family, Pops? You, Laila, Tammy, Nana—you've never missed one of my games."

Camron stopped and turned to face him. He poked a finger into Stephon's chest. "Remember what I always told you."

Stephon repeated it without missing a beat. "You can't take everybody up the mountain, but you bring back what you found on your way up."

Camron nodded. "That's right, son. That's right." Then he broke into a grin. "Speaking of bringing something back—that behind-the-back move today was filthy. You been sneaking looks at my old tapes?"

Stephon burst out laughing. "Whatever, old man. My bag's way deeper than yours ever was."

Their laughter echoed through the darkened warehouse as they disappeared into the night.

A late afternoon car ride brought the family back to Memphis just as dusk draped itself across the Bluff City. Camron barely slowed down—he hustled the family home before he needed to speed off to clock in at his second job, driving a forklift at a warehouse in North Memphis. Between that and fixing A/C units during the day, he scraped together enough to lease a place in Chickasaw Gardens. His kids wouldn't slip through the cracks. History wouldn't repeat itself.

"Order some pizza for dinner, Laila," Camron called as they climbed the wide front porch. "And save a few slices for me." He pointed at Stephon with a grin. "I'm talking to you, Steph," before peeling off down the driveway.

"Why he always trust you with the money?" Tammy grumbled, side-eyeing Laila as she opened the door.

"Because I'm the oldest, and he wants change back when he gets home," Laila shot back.

Tammy rolled her eyes so hard they nearly stuck. She hung her purse on the coat rack with a huff. "Don't nobody want no pizza again."

"Speak for yourself," Stephon muttered. He was already halfway to his room, dropping his bag with a soft thud.

His bedroom was a shrine to basketball. The walls were plastered with Slam magazine covers, posters of his favorite NBA players, and his father's high school basketball jersey. Baller Circuit trophies lined his dresser.

Stephon flopped onto the mattress, feeling every ounce of tension drain from his body. The weight of living up to expectations—plus hours of travel—finally peeled off him. For a moment, it was just relief. A knock on the door cut that short.

"Pizza's here already?" he called out, hopeful.

"Nope." Laila's voice carried a smirk. "Someone's here to see you."

The frame of a wheelchair squeezed awkwardly into the room, a medium gym bag balanced on its owner's lap. Stats—Stephon's best friend since elementary school. Their fathers grew up together and had been tight back in the day, hoping their boys would be the same. Biweekly Saturday sleepovers sealed that deal a long time ago. Stats was the brother Stephon never had.

"Damn," Stephon grinned, "I almost forgot what day it was."

"Hard to keep track when you're out traveling the world, huh superstar?" Stats joked.

"Man, whatever." Stephon laughed, then scrambled to clear clutter from the spare twin bed on the other side of the room—the one always reserved for Stats. He wheeled Stats over, then hoisted him up with a grunt, settling him onto the mattress. "Bro, I swear, lay off the Crumpies."

"You just been skipping the weight room," Stats fired back, the two cracking up as they hugged it out.

That night, same as always, they ate pizza and drank cheap soda, while watching random YouTube clips and battling on NBA 2K. Their loud bursts of laughter earned muffled curses from Laila and Tammy more than once.

Stats could break down any game, any era, like a scholar. Despite what his legs couldn't do, his mind lived in sports. He listened closely as Stephon dissected every quarter of his championship run, chiming in with pointers and insights. Stephon valued that more than he'd ever admit. Stats lived through him, and Stephon thrived on it.

When they finally powered down their phones and pulled the covers up, the mood shifted, the room growing heavy.

"I'm gonna miss this when you leave for Florida," Stats said quietly. His voice cracked at the edges. "Feels like... our last summer."

Stephon let it hang there for a second, thinking about his father's words. Then he reached across and bumped Stats' fist.

"No matter what, bro. Brothers for life."

CHAPTER 1

Secrets

At 7:30 a.m., the bell rang at Martin Luther King Prepatory High School, and a flood of students poured out of classrooms into the hallways, loudly navigating to their next classes. Stephon slammed his locker shut, his 6'4" frame casting a shadow over the chaos of students weaving through the hallway. At sixteen, he moved through the crowd like a giant among ants—locs swaying, mustache catching the fluorescent light, Key Glock's bass line pounding through his AirPods. The world blurred into background noise until something cold and hard pressed against the back of his legs, jerking him from his zone.

"Stats, I know that's you, my nigga," Stephon smiled as he slowly turned around.

"How'd you guess?" said Stats.

"Heard your wheels squeaking a mile away, my guy," Stephon chuckled.

"You're green as hell for that," Stats laughed.

Stephon leaned down and gave Stats a pound-hug. Stats wore a Memphis Tigers fitted hat over his shaved head and wire-framed glasses.

"You watch the game last night?" Stats asked.

"What game?" Stephon replied.

"Titans won. Cam threw for 317 yards, two touchdowns, and no interceptions. Guess what his QBR was?"

Stephon looked down at Stats quizzically. "His what?"

Stats rolled his eyes in frustration. "Total quarterback rating. Never mind. Pollard ran for 152 yards on just 21 carries. That's over seven yards per carry!"

"Listen, Stephen A. Smith, did you do Mr. Branton's homework?"

Stats rolled his eyes and pulled out his phone. In seconds, he sent an email to Stephon with a completed assignment. "You know I just put this in ChatGPT, right? You can do this yourself. It takes a few minutes."

"Why would I do that when I have a friend with a computer for a brain?" Stephon scoffed and gently punched Stats on the shoulder.

A brief silence followed. "How you and your sisters holding up though?" Stats' voice filled with concern. "I still can't believe he's gone."

"I'll be right back." Stephon blurted out, ignoring Stats as he turned around, headed in the other direction and removed his backpack Stephon's locker was at the end of a hall where very few students or teachers visited. Stats noticed Stephon from afar, huddled over his backpack and looking over his shoulder. Stephon looked around, reach inside his bag, and stuffed something into his locker before rushing back to catch up with him.

"We keeping secrets now?" Stats asked as Stephon wheeled him down the hall in a sprint.

Stephon ignored Stats. "We late, let's get to class."

THREE DAYS EARLIER

With dusk falling, Stephon dribbled a basketball on a patch of dirt and brown grass behind his grandmother's house. He dripped with sweat as he crossed over an imaginary defender. The small plot of land behind his grandmother's shotgun house now served as the only place Stephon could be alone. It was where he came morning and night to escape his own thoughts.

His grandmother's house had three bedrooms. She slept in one, Tammy and her two children slept in another, while Stephon slept in the smallest room. Laila, was away at college in Atlanta for her junior year. Stephon had always loved coming here for Sunday dinners—his dad, grandmother, and him packed around the TV, shouting at missed tackles like the receivers could hear them. Fried chicken, collard greens, black-eyed peas, sweet cornbread, cold lemonade. Sundays used to fly by too fast.

Now every day stretched on forever.

This house wasn't the Sunday paradise of his childhood. It was creaky floors, a leaking roof, sudden bursts of gunfire that made you flinch. Nights brought random critters scuttling away when he flicked on the bathroom light. This was still Grandma's house. Just not the version he remembered.

Stephon stared at the rim, crouched over in triple-threat position. He closed his eyes and saw flashbacks of his childhood with his father guarding him, encouraging Stephon to attack the rim. When his eyes opened, he saw his sister Tammy standing in his path to the rim with her hands on her hips. She was tall and slender, with an oversized vintage 2Pac shirt draped over black spandex tights.

"You know these walls ain't soundproof, right?"

"My bad, Tammy. Did I wake up the boys?"

Stephon glanced over at the bedroom window and saw his nephews peeping out at them through the blinds. Tammy rolled her eyes.

"You talked to Laila?" Stephon changed the subject.

"I ain't heard from your sister since she left for college this semester."

"Why you say it like that? She your sister too."

"Listen, Laila is all about political science and law school now, and I'm all about making sure these kids eat, you stay in school, and granny's diabetes doesn't get any worse."

"Y'all still going back and forth. We family. Dad wouldn't have that shit."

"Well, he ain't here . . . so."

A Tiffany blue Mercedes S-Class crunched into the driveway, chrome rims glinting in the sunlight. Stephon didn't recognize the ride. Dolce and Gabbana tennis shoes hit the gravel as the driver emerged—TK, Tammy's latest boyfriend. Short and wiry with a fresh taper fade, he strutted toward the backyard, designer shades hiding his eyes. Sweet marijuana smoke trailed from his vape pen. Tattoo sleeves covered his arms, and the unmistakable outline of a semi-automatic pressed against his shirt as he moved, appearing and disappearing with each step.

"Shit, TK's here already," Tammy said. "Listen, I'm about to go out. Can you watch the boys for me?"

"Aight," Stephon responded as he released a high-arching shot over Tammy's head. The net snapped behind her.

TK approached the backyard as Tammy scurried away to get dressed. "I'll be ready in 5 minutes, TK. Wait out here with Steph." Stephon nodded to TK but didn't speak. He grabbed his rubber evolution ball from the grass and started his routine back up.

"You hooping, ain't you?" TK said as he smirked and held his hands out, signaling to Stephon to pass him the ball for a shot. Stephon tossed the ball to him reluctantly. TK caught it and chucked up a pitiful attempt towards the goal. The ball soared well over the rim, missing everything.

"I see you ain't," Stephon laughed as he chased the errant shot.

"You're right, but I am balling though." TK pulled at his Cuban link.

"Dealing isn't my thing," Stephon responded.

"Dealing?" TK scoffed. TK waved Stephon over. "Let me show you something." Stephon hesitated before walking towards him. TK whipped out his phone and opened an application showing multiple stock investments. "Crypto, my boy, not crack. This ain't the '80s. Put a thousand on bitcoin back when it was going for the low."

Stephon's eyebrows raised when he saw the amount. "Damn. That's a lot of zeros." He took another shot and swished it. "If you're not in the streets, why are you toting a gun?"

"This is still Memphis, my nigga." TK asked for another shot. "Listen, if these hoop dreams don't pan out, holler at me. I'm pulling in 20k a month trading."

"Bet," Stephon replied.

Stephon kept shooting when he noticed a teenager nicknamed Q and a group of three young men passing by his front yard. Q was a part of the Frayser Fiends, a neighborhood gang that was notoriously violent. Stephon and Q exchanged menacing looks as the group passed. TK noticed the exchange.

"What's up with that?" TK asked.

"Dude who likes Laila. Had to knock him out a while back for talking crazy to her. Been beefing ever since, and now we're at the same school."

TK held the ball and spun it twice before tossing another horrible shot towards the basket.

"I got something I want to show you," TK remarked.

Then he went to his car and grabbed something from the trunk. He handed it to Stephon and asked, "You can keep a secret, right?"

CHAPTER 2

Misfits

Tim, MLK's athletic director, sat on the couch in Principal Davenport's office, dumping a bag of hot Cheetos into his mouth. He was a 31-year-old white man wearing a polo shirt with an MLK mascot embroidered on the chest. A black whistle hung from his neck.

"I can't believe you still eat those," Principal Davenport shook her head in disbelief. "You know those things are going to kill you, right?"

"We all have our vices," Tim retorted as he licked his powdery-red fingers dry.

Principal Davenport shook her head disapprovingly. "What are we going to do about this coaching situation? As much as I appreciate you taking over mid-season last year, you're not exactly cut out for coaching. No disrespect."

"None taken." Tim tossed the empty bag of hot Cheetos in the trash.

"What do you know about this new transfer, Stephon Johnson? Not often do we see star athletes transfer from prep school to public."

"His dad died recently. The kid was nationally ranked. He moved back in with his grandmother and sister after the funeral.

Now he's here." Tim plopped down on the couch. "But word is, he doesn't play competitively anymore."

Principal Davenport shook her head in disbelief. "What about last year's team?"

Tim rose from the couch and nodded his head towards the door. "Walk with me for a second," he asked.

The two walked out of Principal Davenport's office, down the hall, and towards the gymnasium. It was lunchtime, and the halls were empty, save for a group of students playing and watching an unauthorized game of pickup ball. Principal Davenport and Tim peered through the gym door.

They watched as ten mostly shirtless young men ran up and down the court, playing a frenzied game of five on five. Airballs, turnovers, and missed layups riddled the game. Principal Davenport recognized all of the young men—six of them were players on last year's 5-15 team. The others were wannabe athletes who barely showed up for school and cut class whenever they did.

Tim whispered while pointing out certain players. "Where should I start? You've got Tavon Graham. Talented but hot-tempered. Curses like a sailor, and he's been suspended a bunch of times for fighting."

As Tim spoke, Tavon lashed out at one of his teammates to pass him the ball.

"Oh, and you see the kid walking up and down the court not getting back on defense? Terrence Price. Good kid; comes from a hardworking family. But he can't keep the girls off him. Had two of them fighting over him in gym class yesterday." Tim scoffed as he pointed at a group of girls sitting high in the bleachers giggling. "Kid has a ton of talent but too many distractions."

"Oh, and then you've got DaRon Scott . . ." Tim scoffed before Principal Davenport cut him off.

" . . . Mom is a former addict working doubles as a traveling nurse. Barely home. The kid works a job at night to keep the lights on," Principal Davenport interjected. "I know all their stories, Tim. I need answers, not biographies."

"Katrina, with all due respect, Coach Carter couldn't help these kids. They're a bunch of misfits," Tim sighed.

Just as Tim uttered these words, a shouting match broke out between Tavon and DaRon over a hard foul.

"This ain't prison, bruh. All that hacking ain't necessary," Tavon yelled.

"Get your man, Terrence, before I beat the breaks off em," DaRon replied flippantly.

Tavon started towards DaRon with clenched fists when Principal Davenport and Tim rushed into the gym, shutting the game down and telling everyone to go to class. The players all grumbled under their breath and collected their belongings. When the last person left the gym, Principal Davenport picked up an abandoned basketball and began shooting free throws. Tim rebounded for her.

"You might be right," said Principal Davenport after swishing her fourth free throw in a row. "Who on earth would sign up to coach these kids?"

Tim held the ball for a while and shook his head before throwing a chest pass. "I'm working on it." Principal Davenport caught the ball with a dubious look and sank another.

CHAPTER 3

Things Fall Apart

Principal Davenport's office at MLK was a shrine to order and cleanliness. The books on her bookshelf were in neat rows, organized in alphabetical order by author. Her desk was meticulously organized, with pencils and pens arranged by color. Artwork on the wall hung symmetrically. Everything had its place. The walls showcased two framed degrees that hung proudly side by side: her undergraduate degree from Howard University and her master's degree from Vanderbilt University. The carpet was freshly vacuumed. A diffuser provided the room with the pleasant smell of lemongrass.

Principal Davenport fixed her gaze in a standing mirror near her desk. She was an attractive, brown-skinned woman with a short, trendy haircut and a well-fitted pinstripe suit that accentuated her athletic build. She sat back in her office chair, reading through students' files when she heard a knock at the door. It was Tim returning from cafeteria duty. He cradled a half-dozen box of Gibson doughnuts in his right hand and plopped down on the leather sofa across from Principal Davenport's desk.

"Have a seat, Tim," Principal Davenport gestured sarcastically to the couch.

"Doughnut?" Tim asked.

"I thought you were on a diet?" Principal Davenport replied.

"I was... last week," Tim answered, scoffing down a glazed circle. "Anyway, whatchu over there reading?"

Principal Davenport shook her head. "Student files." She raised a stack of files and slapped them on her desk one by one after each word. "Neglect. Food insecurity. Abuse. Single parents. Twenty percent of the student body has an IEP."

She stood up and stared out the window. "You know, back in the day, this school graduated some of the most talented folks in the country—Maurice White, W.W. Herrington, Marion Barry."

As Principal Davenport continued, a notification vibrated from Tim's phone.

"I hate to interrupt the trip down memory lane... but," Tim interjected.

"But what?" Principal Davenport responded with frustration.

Tim stood up from the couch and walked over to Principal Davenport to show her a message from an unknown number on his phone.

TEXT: Check locker 102. A gun is in it.

Principal Davenport jumped up from her desk, grabbed her suit coat, and the two rushed out together.

Meanwhile, in a classroom on the second floor, Mr. Branton sat cross-legged on his desk, facing his class. He wore a colorful dashiki, and his long locs were covered in a tam. He held up a worn copy of *Things Fall Apart.*

"What did Okonkwo mean when he said, 'Living fire begets cold, impotent ash?'" Mr. Branton asked.

The class of thirty students made no eye contact with Mr. Branton, and no one volunteered. "Mr. Johnson, what are your thoughts?" Mr. Branton asked Stephon, who was daydreaming in the back of the class.

Before Stephon could answer, Officer Booker, MLK's security, strutted into the classroom. He was a hulking man, tall and wide with a barrel chest. He chewed on a toothpick and glared at the students.

"Can I help you, Officer Booker?" Mr. Branton asked, irritated at the disruption.

"I need to see Stephon Johnson," Officer Booker replied in his gravelly voice.

The students all turned to face Stephon, who sat upright in his seat.

"What did I do?" he asked.

"In the hallway," Mr. Branton said. "This is already taking up too much of my class time."

Officer Booker motioned for Stephon. "Let's go, son."

In the hallway, Stephon sheepishly trailed Officer Booker. He was nervous, and his face showed it. "What did I do?" Stephon asked.

"I ask the questions, not you," Officer Booker snapped.

Officer Booker continued walking, and Stephon followed him. Officer Booker stopped at Stephon's locker, where the school's janitor leaned against the lockers, holding a pair of bolt cutters. The three of them could hear the clicks of Principal Davenport's heels echoing from around the corner as they waited near the locker.

Principal Davenport turned the corner and emerged into the hallway. "Hello, Mr. Johnson," she said as she reached the waiting group. "102 is your locker?"

"Um, yes, ma'am," Stephon stammered.

"An anonymous source reported that you are storing weapons in your locker. Is that true?"

"Weapons?" Stephon sounded shocked. "What?! I don't have weapons in my locker."

"A gun," Officer Booker interjected, leaning into Stephon, nearly face to face. "You got a gun in there?"

Principal Davenport shot Officer Booker a glare. He noticed, acknowledged it silently, and took a step back.

"Is there a gun in your locker, Mr. Johnson?" Principal Davenport asked.

"Nothing in there but books," Stephon replied. "I ain't got no gun. Somebody lied."

Principal Davenport rubbed her palms together. "Will you open your locker and allow Officer Booker to search it? If not, we will open it with the bolt cutters."

Stephon slowly rotated the combination lock on his locker. His heart raced. Sweat began to build on his forehead. He removed the lock and slowly opened the door.

BACK IN HER OFFICE

Principal Davenport had her door shut and lay on her couch alone. Her eyes were closed and filled with tears as she meditated. Suddenly, she received a call from the front desk.

"Principal Davenport, the police are here to take Stephon Johnson into custody," said the receptionist.

"Tell them I'll be out in a second."

She pulled out the photo—her father in his pastor's robe, the one she'd carried through every impossible decision. Three years since cancer took him, but their conversations never stopped. Her fingers traced the worn edges as she whispered a prayer. Sending one of her students to jail felt like betrayal, but what choice did she have?

She steeled herself and stepped into the waiting room. Officers circled Stephon like vultures, his massive frame somehow diminished by the handcuffs biting into his wrists. One cop held up a black gun sealed in a zip-tie bag like a trophy. Stephon's eyes were glassy with unshed tears.

"That gun ain't mine, Principal Davenport. I'm telling the truth," Stephon pleaded.

"Then how did it get there? Did you give anyone your combination? Give me something, Stephon."

"I don't know, but I'm telling you the truth."

"Then I don't have much of a choice."

The group of officers began walking Stephon out of the principal's office as he started to jerk away and struggle. The officers grabbed him and restricted his movement down the hallway as students gawked and gossiped. Stephon kept his head down but looked up briefly when he noticed Stats seated in his wheelchair near the exit. The two exchanged looks of worry before he was stuffed into a squad car and driven away.

CHAPTER 4

Memphis Blues

Nas' words hit Lenny Chase hard—Iron Mike hard. They always had. "Drunk By Myself" was his favorite song to listen to when he returned home to his only form of meditation—in control, behind the wheel, weaving through Memphis streets, headed to see familiar faces at Sunnybrook. Now, after returning home from a career playing overseas, he needed the drive more than ever.

The vibration of Lenny's iPhone sitting in his car's cup holder awoke him from his nostalgia. A photo of his agent and longtime friend, A.J., appeared on the caller ID. A.J. was one of Lenny's teammates in college. He played in the NBA for two years before becoming a full-time agent. He knew early on that basketball wasn't going to pay the bills forever and started to focus on the business of sports instead.

Lenny turned the music down, his heart racing in anticipation of hearing which NBA team had called.

"A.J., what's good!?"

"Len, I got some bad news, my guy. I spoke with the Celtics. They liked your workout, but . . ."

"But what?"

"You didn't make the cut, bro. Sorry."

Lenny ended the call. He pulled into Sunnybrook's pothole-riddled parking lot. He purposefully took up two parking spaces, turned off the ignition, and slouched back in his seat, exhaling a forceful breath of disappointment and anger.

The Celtics tryout felt different—electric. Lenny was in the zone, jump shot after jump shot swishing through the net without touching iron. Brad Stevens watched from the stands as Lenny moved like liquid, his defense suffocating, every drill executed to perfection.

This was it. His ticket back home.

But perfect wasn't enough. Again.

The rejection hit like a sledgehammer. Another year overseas stretched ahead of him, another year of trying to fit into cultures that felt foreign no matter how hard he smiled or learned the language. The loneliness had already started eating him alive in Italy—weekend drinks at empty bars turned into weekday escapes, then daily necessity. The final straw came when he showed up drunk to a game and threw a punch at the referee. Kicked off the team, reputation in shambles.

The NBA wasn't just a dream anymore—it was salvation. His only shot at getting back to the States, back to himself, back to the man he used to be before the isolation swallowed him whole.

He reached into his console and grabbed a silver-colored flask filled with Remy. He drained it in just a few chugs.

♪♪

I don't want none of my peeps caught up in none of my beef

I'mma ride to the end of the road if I have to

Praying no car speeds by for me to crash to

♪♪

Lenny pushed out of his car and walked up to one of the oldest bars in the city. A tattered canopy with the words "World's Famous Sunnybrook on Beale Street" hung over grimy storefront windows, with fluorescent logos of the Memphis Tigers and Budweiser attached.

Sunnybrook burst onto Beale Street in 1950, its neon sign beckoning musicians with calloused fingers and dreams bigger than their pockets. By the late fifties, the bar had become sacred ground—a refuge where working-class black folks could shed the weight of Jim Crow's suffocating grip and breathe freely.

Inside those smoky walls, a different world existed. Here, a janitor could become a king behind a microphone, a seamstress could dance until her feet forgot the factory floor, and laughter drowned out the cruel whispers of a segregated city. Sunnybrook wasn't just a bar—it was sanctuary, defiance, and hope wrapped in blues riffs and bourbon.

At Sunnybrook, social status meant nothing. Whether you shined shoes at the Peabody Hotel or were a practicing lawyer at 201 Poplar defending criminals from prosecution, Sunnybrook welcomed you. The drinks were cheap, the patrons were Black, and the music never stopped.

Lenny entered the bar and was met by Howlin' Wolf's "Little Red Rooster" blaring from a corner jukebox. The bar smelled like body odor, stale beer, and desperation.

In 60 years, Sunnybrook hadn't changed much. The same photos of MLK, Malcolm X, and B.B. King were displayed on the walls alongside newer portraits of Larry Finch, Penny Hardaway, and Lorenzen Wright. As Lenny made his way to the end of the bar, he noticed the same familiar faces chasing shots of liquor with somber thoughts of dashed dreams and regrets—and the same owner, Cliff Bell. Cliff owned and operated Sunnybrook since it was passed down to him by his father, Ray. Ray purchased Sunnybrook with life insurance proceeds after his father's death in 1950—a man who believed in Black-owned business.

"Don't be like the rest of these Black folks and leave your kids with nothing when you die, Cliff. Build something for yourself, son. Ya hear me?" Ray always said.

Lenny spotted Cliff standing at the far end of the bar, with his back turned toward the customers, polishing glasses. The old man stood 6'6", 260 pounds, with broad shoulders set atop a portly core. He wore linen trousers and an open-collared silk bowling shirt. A gold Cuban link chain hung around his neck.

Lenny walked over and pulled up a seat at the bar. He noticed the imprint of the pearl-handled .38 special Cliff kept in the back of his waistband to settle differences. "I see you over there pretending like you working. You ain't fooling nobody."

Cliff turned around slowly, trying to guess the voice behind him. "Young blood!" Cliff exclaimed when he saw it was Lenny. The two clasped hands, pulling one another in together tightly. Cliff stood back and smiled.

"Whatcha doing in town? I thought you were somewhere in Europe shooting that ball."

"Back home. At least for a little."

"Man, good to see you," Cliff said. "I got something special for you." Cliff walked to the back of the bar and pushed through double swinging doors that led to the kitchen. When he returned, he was holding a bottle of Remy XO.

"Damn, Coach C, you know you ain't gotta pull the good stuff out for me."

"Bullshit, you know I'mma hook you up when you come in town, Len. Ain't no problem at all. I haven't seen you in years." Cliff twisted open the bottle of Remy and poured Lenny a full glass.

Cliff's son, Zo, grew up in the same neighborhood as Lenny. Cliff coached them both in AAU until they were thirteen. The two were perfect teammates. Zo's unstoppable post-game perfectly complemented Lenny's silky-smooth jumper. They won nationals two years in a row. Most people predicted the two would play together in high school, but fate had different plans.

Cliff was unapologetically abrasive. The yelling, the cursing, the lack of emotion came down like an avalanche on Zo's mother over the years. She filed for divorce, and the court granted her custody of Zo. Zo's mother sent him to Briershire, a private school. Lenny could only afford the yellow bus ride to MLK to play for Coach Heard, and so Lenny and Zo were teammates no more. The two continued their friendship throughout high school, calling each other after games and meeting up when they could on weekends to catch up at the mall, dreaming about their futures in the NBA.

Twenty minutes later, while Lenny sipped the expensive cognac and Cliff sipped coffee, a memory struck Cliff and made him smile.

"Remember that game in '05?" Cliff asked. "You versus Zo? Man, people still talk about that game 'til this day."

MEMPHIS 2005

Every year, Melrose High School plays host to the season-opening MLK tournament. The contest offers public schools the rare opportunity to match up against their private counterparts for bragging rights. The 2005 tournament championship showcased the long-awaited matchup between Zo and Lenny, who, at the time, were high school seniors ranked #1 and #2 in the state, respectively.

The entire Orange Mound community wrapped around the building to see the most anticipated game of the season. Tickets sold out hours before the game, but that didn't stop people from trying to force their way inside.

Inside the gym, police struggled to keep the crowds from spilling onto the court as the 2,000 seats quickly filled up and the game became standing room only.

Playa Fly's "Nobody Needs Nobody" exploded through the speakers, bass lines vibrating through the floorboards as Lenny's team jogged into the layup line. The crowd erupted like this was their house, not neutral ground. Every seat packed, every voice raised—this wasn't just another game.

MLK versus Briershire. The matchup said everything about Memphis without saying a word.

On one side stood Martin Luther King Jr. Preparatory—named for a legend, built from necessity, representing every dream that systemic racism tried to crush. Their players carried the weight of neighborhoods forgotten by city planners, schools starved of resources, futures that required twice the work for half the recognition.

Across the court: Briershire Academy. Born as a "segregation academy" in the shadow of Brown v. Board, designed to keep white students from ever sharing a classroom with black ones. Better facilities, better teachers, better everything—except character.

This wasn't Lenny versus Zo. This was history colliding at center court.

The entire city of Memphis rallied behind Lenny, and although they respected Zo, he had become an outsider. The game tipped off. Thirty minutes of basketball flew by, and only two minutes remained in the fourth quarter. Lenny had 30 points, 8 assists, and 5 steals. Zo had notched 20 points, 15 rebounds, and 4 blocks. MLK led the game by 3.

Clock bleeding down. Briershire's point guard zipped the ball to Zo on the block—exactly where Coach Heard knew it was going. The double team came flying from the weak side, just like it had all night. But this time, Zo was ready. He pivoted, ball cocked high above his head, reading both defenders like a book. In one fluid motion, he whipped a laser pass across court to the opposite corner—a perfect strike to his wide-open teammate. The shooter caught it clean, elevated over the desperate dive of an MLK defender, and let it fly. The ball hung in the air like a prayer.

Swish.

Dead tie. Everything on the line.

Lenny's teammate grabbed the ball and inbounded it to Lenny. Lenny dribbled the ball toward half court, looking to Coach Heard to see if he wanted a timeout. But Coach Heard shook his head, signaling to Lenny that when he crossed half court, he should take the final shot.

The gym had exploded into pandemonium—feet stomping bleachers, voices crashing together in a wall of sound. Fifteen seconds. Zo abandoned his man and slid in front of Lenny, eye to eye for the final dance.

Lenny worked the ball between his legs, each dribble deliberate as he crept toward the key. Zo knew what was coming—he'd seen this movie before. AAU 13-and-under championship. Same setup, same killer instinct. Cross left, step back, game over.

Seven seconds. Lenny made his move, exploding right then cutting back left. The step-back came just like Zo remembered, but this time he was ready. His hand slapped ball, sending it careening toward half-court where a Briershire player scooped it up. One dribble. A desperate heave from two steps past the logo.

The buzzer screamed. The ball found nothing but net.

Briershire players poured onto the court like a flood, celebration drowning out MLK's stunned silence. Same story, different day— privilege always found a way to win.

PRESENT DAY

"Yeah, Coach, crazy game. When's the last time you talked to Zo?"

Cliff shook his head. "Man, I haven't seen or heard from that boy in years."

Two customers began loudly arguing at the other end of the bar. Cliff grimaced. "Let me deal with these fools. I'll be back."

Lenny took another shot. When he looked up, he noticed a white man walking toward him. His face was hidden by a Memphis Tigers fitted hat. A gray cut-off sleeve revealed an assortment of tattoos. As the man drew closer, Lenny recognized him as Tim, his former teammate at MLK.

Tim was the lone white face in a sea of black and brown—had been since elementary school. His father Peter still owned the house directly across from MLK Prep, the same cracked driveway where Tim had learned to shoot hoops and navigate two worlds.

Peter was old-school blue-collar, hands still scarred from factory work and war. When Lenny came over after school to demolish Tim at video games, Peter would inevitably drift into his Vietnam stories. Always the same one: his black squadmate diving onto a landmine, saving the whole platoon. The blast that sent shrapnel tearing through Peter's face, costing him half an ear but teaching him everything about brotherhood.

"Real brothers don't give a damn what color you are," Peter would say, unconsciously touching the mangled side of his head. "And neither does your enemy."

The lesson stuck. Tim knew he belonged here not because he was different, but because difference didn't matter when it counted.

Tim stopped when his eyes met Lenny's, and they shared a smile of recognition. Tim's voice was nearly a yell. "Len, what's good! I haven't seen you in forever, fam." Lenny smiled and extended his hand for Tim to shake, but Tim surprised him with a bear hug. Tim sat next to Lenny.

Lenny chuckled. Tim had always been a hugger and still was. "Tim, it's been a minute. Catch me up."

"Been longer than a minute. It's been years!"

"You're right. I'm bad at staying in contact."

Tim snickered. "Bad? You're terrible!" They both laughed.

Lenny nodded in acknowledgment. "Well, how have you been then?"

"I'm great. Married Niesha. Got two boys, 11 and 8. And you wouldn't believe it, but I'm the Athletic Director at MLK now."

"Congrats, man. On all of it."

"Thanks. You know your girl is the principal over there."

"Who?"

"Who? Come on now, you know who? Katrina. The girl you've loved since middle school. That's who."

"I knew she was teaching a while ago, but the principal?"

"Yeah, man, she still looks good too."

Lenny gazed into the bottom of his shot glass, swirling the Remy around in a circle for a few seconds before downing it.

"Is that your Challenger outside? I see you, big money."

"Man, I wish. Just taking it one day at a time, bro."

"Well, how long are you in town for?"

Lenny shrugged. "I'm thinking about staying."

Tim's eyes lit up. "You ever thought about coaching?"

Lenny responded too quickly. "Coaching isn't for me."

"You're right." Tim nodded. "It's for the kids."

Cliff walked over and rested his elbows on the bar. "Tim, didn't you see the 'no loitering' sign? This ain't a Starbucks."

Tim smiled and nodded. "Lemme get a Ghost River."

Cliff nodded, filled a mug with beer, and slid it over to Tim. "Closing down soon, boys, so drink up." Cliff walked over to another waiting customer.

Tim raised his beer mug in salute. "To Lenny Chase, the best to ever come out of MLK?"

"Thinking about visiting Coach Heard's gravesite soon," Lenny blurted out, changing the subject. His face turned sullen.

After an awkward moment, Tim took another sip of his beer. "The funeral was beautiful," he said. "Wish you could have been there."

"Yeah, me too." Lenny finished his sixth shot of Remy in one gulp. He pushed back from the bar and walked over to the rectangular wooden jukebox with an arched top. He pulled a quarter from his pocket and placed it in the machine. After flipping through the selection of albums, he pressed 249 on the box: Memphis Blues by W.C. Handy. It was his father's favorite song.

CHAPTER 5

Sorry Coach

L enny Chase pulled his matte black Dodge Challenger into the vacant parking lot of Mt. Zion Christian Cemetery, Memphis's largest African American gravesite. Mt. Zion's 32 acres served as the city's final resting place for over 30,000 Memphians. Locals still joked that Zion is the "one place in Memphis where everybody gets along."

Lenny killed the engine and sat back, exhaling deeply. He turned down a Young Dolph song bumping through the speakers. He reached into the glove compartment and pulled out a half-drunk pint of Remy Martin. He poured what remained of the pint into a plastic Faygo bottle and gently swirled it. He took a swig, then another. The warmth calmed him. He took one more swig before sliding out of the car.

It was an unseasonably cool day. There was a slight breeze that felt more like fall than summer. The smell of damp soil and weathered headstones filled the air. Tall blades of Kentucky bluegrass danced in the wind. Day was turning into night, and the sky brimmed with a blue hue.

Lenny navigated the maze of graves and eventually found Coach Heard's. The headstone, once smooth granite, was now weathered and filled with cracks. Carved into the face of the headstone were the words "Phillip Heard" with "Gone but not forgotten" etched underneath.

Lenny stood over the gravesite and touched the cold granite headstone with his left hand while pouring out part of his Remy Martin onto the grass. He propped the near-empty Faygo bottle atop the headstone and pulled a single folded sheet of paper from his back pocket. He unraveled the note, took a deep breath, and began to read it:

Dear Coach:

When my father died, I didn't feel anything because I never got the chance to know him well enough to miss him. Although I was physically present for his funeral, I was mentally in another place. The opposite is true for you, Coach. I'm sorry I didn't visit you in the hospital. To be honest, basketball overseas was just my excuse to avoid seeing you laid up in some bed with tubes sticking out of your body like some science experiment.

You are the strongest man I've ever known, and I always wanted to remember you that way. My mom didn't speak to me for a week when I missed the funeral, but when I told her that I didn't want anyone else around when I said my goodbyes, she said she understood. I hope you understand too.

[Lenny took the liquor-filled Faygo bottle to the head and continued reading]

I'm still striving to become the man you believed I could be. I knew I would not be able to muster the strength to read this at your funeral, so I wanted to deliver it to you myself.

I'm sorry, Coach. You gave me more than I can ever repay. But maybe one day.

Love,

Len

Lenny wiped tears from his eyes as he searched for a rock on the ground. When he found one, he took the letter and placed the rock on top of it in front of Coach Heard's grave.

CHAPTER 6

All We Got

The brown Ford Explorer cut through the Friday afternoon heat, flying south on I-75 toward Florida. 2Pac's voice filled the cab—"Me Against the World"—as Stephon rode shotgun, watching the miles disappear. His father Camron gripped the wheel, both of them knowing this drive would change everything.

Stephon's mind raced faster than the highway rushing beneath them. One of the nation's top prep schools. Elite competition coast to coast. Division 1 scouts in every gym. Those brutal 5 AM workouts, the late-night drills that left his legs screaming—every drop of sweat had led to this moment. The scholarship was practically guaranteed now.

He rolled down the window and let the summer air hit his face, tasting freedom.

"Remember, don't get caught up in any mess down there in Florida. Books and basketball. That's it."

"I gotcha, pops," Stephon responded nonchalantly.

"I'm serious. It ain't like when I was coming up. Y'all got way more distractions than we had..."

Stephon heard the loud screech of tires cut off his father's sentence. Stephon screamed as an eighteen-wheeler jackknifed two cars ahead of them, striking a silver Chevy Caprice in front of their Explorer. Cam made a hard turn of the wheel to avoid colliding with the Caprice and careened into the side rail. The memory went dark.

PRESENT DAY

Stephon jolted awake, cold sweat streaming down his face. The nightmare again—always the same, always ending with his father's blood on hot asphalt. His heart hammered against his ribs as reality crashed back.

No NBA posters. No bedroom in South Memphis. Just the dingy white ceiling of Tall Trees Detention Center staring back at him like a dead eye. He'd replayed that scene hundreds of times but waking up never got easier. The razor-thin sheet clung to his chest as he sat up on the top bunk, and a voice drifted up from below.

"My boy, you been tussling all night. You good?"

Stephon rolled towards the edge of the bed and looked down at his bunkmate below. "My bad, bruh."

"Haha, I'm just messing with you, man. What's your name?"

"Steph."

"Like Curry, huh? I'm D-Lo." A brief silence ensued. "First night is the worst, but you get used to it."

"Man, I don't see how," Steph mumbled.

"Just don't start nothing with nobody, and you'll be straight. Keep your head down and your eyes open."

Stephon continued staring at the ceiling as his eyes began to water. He had no idea what time it was. No idea if his sisters were coming for him. No idea if D-Lo was in for shoplifting or murder. No idea if he would ever leave.

Almost on cue, D-Lo broke the silence. "You don't need to worry about me, but I can't say the same for them folks out there," D-Lo noted. D-Lo got up from his bed and headed to use the combination sink and toilet. He noticed Stephon staring at his Memphis Lords gang tattoo spanning his shoulder blades.

"You bang?" D-Lo asked.

"Naw, my dad ran with the Lords back in the day," Stephon explained, hoping to build rapport. "Cam Johnson."

"What!? Your dad was a real O.G. back in the day. My big brother used to tell me stories about him."

Stephon turned over in his bed and stared at the wall. "He gave that life up when he got out of jail. Turned Muslim. But he died in a car wreck a few months ago."

"Damn, man. Sorry to hear that. Memphis curse, I guess," D-Lo responded as he flushed the toilet and headed back to his bunk. "My momma always said there's a reason this is the birthplace of the blues."

As D-Lo spoke, a white guard with a buzz cut that the inmates called White Chocolate shined a flashlight in D-Lo's face. "D-Lo, you know the rules. Ain't no chit-chat after lights out."

White Chocolate turned off the flashlight, turned his back, and walked away twirling his nightstick. D-Lo waited a few minutes.

"On Fridays, we hoop in the yard," D-Lo whispered. "The guards be betting on the games. Winner gets extra wings at dinner. I hope you know how to hoop."

"I'm done with basketball, man."

D-Lo turned over in his bed towards the wall. "Hate to tell ya, but basketball is all we got in here."

CHAPTER 7

That Fool Hooping

Stephon stood at center court awaiting the tip-off. He had vowed never to play competitive basketball again after his father's death. It was basketball that caused him to lose the most important person in his life. But he couldn't ignore D-Lo's words from the previous night. What else did he have left?

A heavyset guard approached mid-court with a basketball in his right hand and a whistle in his left. Dozens of shirtless juveniles sat on cheap aluminum benches surrounding the court, watching intently. Barbed wire fences enclosed the square. Stephon looked over at the benches and saw his cellmate D-Lo smiling at him.

As the whistle blew, the ball was tipped to the opposing team's point guard, a 6'2" muscular seventeen-year-old in for burglary. He rifled a pass to an open teammate under the rim, who scored the game's first bucket.

Tall Trees had felt like another planet, but the moment Stephon's sneakers hit the court, he was home. A slender forward stood out of bounds beneath the rim, scanning for an outlet. Stephon flashed his hands—the ball snapped to him like it belonged there. His stocky defender lunged forward, but Stephon was already gone, gliding past with a subtle hesitation that left the kid grasping air. Another defender stepped up at the three-point line, arms wide, standing too tall. Mistake. Stephon's dribble went soft left, then exploded hard right between his legs—the defender spun like a turnstile. The lane gaped open. Stephon hit the gas, and a foot inside the free throw line, he launched. Time suspended. His legs spread wide in that iconic Jordan silhouette, the rim rushing up to meet him. The dunk thundered through the gym as voices erupted around him.

For the first time in months, Stephon smiled.

"That fool hoopin!" yelled D-Lo.

Security guards standing on the outskirts with money in hand oohed. White Chocolate clutched his chest, nearly dropping his phone. Stephon completely dominated the game. His jumper was erratic, but he attacked the lane with power and authority. Every dribble, every dunk was an artistic expression. Basketball was therapy.

"Bruh, I've got to record this. This dude is a walking bucket," White Chocolate said to a fellow guard while pulling out his phone.

"20 years here, never seen anything like it," responded the guard.

After the game, people on both teams embraced Stephon with handshakes, fist pumps, and head nods of respect. D-Lo awaited on the sidelines.

"Bruh, you was hooping out the frame. We eating wings tonight!" laughed D-Lo as he gave Stephon a congratulatory slap on the back. Stephon smiled back briefly as his fellow inmates formed an assembly line facing the stainless-steel door leading back into the atrium.

D-Lo walked toward the line as Stephon stood at half court, staring at the empty benches. For a moment, he saw a mirage of his father watching him from the bleachers, nodding his head in approval.

The vision vanished, and he walked back into the detention center.

CHAPTER 8

Poetry Saved My Life

L enny finished drying the dishes from dinner. "Soul Man" by
Sam & Dave was playing from the Amazon Echo that sat on
the countertop. Lenny turned to see his mother swaying to the
music as she wiped down the dining room table.

Dinner was delicious: Tilapia Milanese and penne with vodka
sauce. Lenny's mother, Patricia, was an Italian food aficionado—a
Southern gal with an Italian palate. Patricia served dinner with a
Chianti Classico, and even though Lenny was far from a wine
connoisseur, he appreciated how the vino complemented the meal.

A few summers back, Patricia visited Lenny when he was playing
in Greece. It was Patricia's first trip to Europe, her first trip outside
the United States. When Patricia left Greece, she spent a few days
touring Italy and fell in love with the cuisine. Every city was a new
food discovery for Patricia—a culinary epiphany. The flavors,
textures, and colors gave food a new meaning. After Lenny's father's
death, Patricia cooked for convenience. She was a single working
mom. With work, school, and a son playing in basketball games
nearly every night, she didn't have the luxury of elaborate meal
planning.

After her Euro trip, Patricia signed up for weekend culinary
classes at Southwest Tennessee Community College. She learned
how to read a recipe, quarter and truss a chicken, and the
importance of a paring knife. Most importantly, cooking brought

out Patricia's creativity, which had gone dormant for years due to work, motherhood, and loneliness. Cooking became her passion.

Patricia had insisted that Lenny eat dinner with her and her boyfriend, Eddie. She and Eddie had celebrated their one-year anniversary a week earlier, and she felt their relationship getting stronger. She wanted Lenny and Eddie to begin the slow process of becoming comfortable around each other. Patricia needed Lenny to accept that Eddie was a part of her life for—what she planned to be—a long time.

ONE YEAR PRIOR

Patricia met Eddie at a pastry class held at the Memphis Botanic Garden. Eddie was a retired Memphis police officer. His wife died a few years prior from breast cancer.

After his wife's death, Eddie's diet consisted mainly of Dairy Queen, D'bo's, and other fast food he could easily microwave the next day. After experiencing stroke symptoms, Eddie's doctor advised him to change his diet in a hurry. Eddie never learned to cook; his late wife cooked every meal. So, Eddie started taking cooking classes.

The knife work and seasonings were fine, but what Eddie really craved was the laughter echoing off the kitchen walls. At sixty-five, his social calendar had shrunk to three sacred rituals: monthly golf with his old cop crew at Fox Meadows, Brotherhood poker nights at the Prince Hall Lodge, and endless hours in his recliner watching Clint Eastwood squint through dusty Western showdowns.

For a Few Dollars More still gave him chills, though *The Outlaw Josey Wales* ran a damn close second. But here in this cooking class, surrounded by chatter about grandkids and garden tomatoes, Eddie felt something he'd forgotten—the simple joy of belonging somewhere new.

At each cooking class, Eddie met new people. He made new friends, and he met Patricia. They shared a bond instantly—both Memphis natives, both widows, and both in love with cooking.

PRESENT DAY

Since Lenny's dad's death, Lenny had been the only man in Patricia's life. It would take time for Lenny to accept the new position that Eddie held. Eddie, the self-proclaimed dessert specialist, made tiramisù for dessert. Baking was really his excuse for satisfying his own insatiable sweet tooth.

It was a warm, moonless night. Patricia lived in a modest house on a quiet street off Riverside. This wasn't the house Lenny grew up in. After Lenny's father's death, Patricia finished her undergraduate degree in education at LeMoyne–Owen College so she could better provide for Lenny and herself. She began her teaching career with Memphis City Schools and was just a few years away from her twentieth anniversary as an elementary school teacher.

After dinner, Lenny walked out of the house and sat on the hood of his car. He needed the escape. Ever since he returned home, Patricia peppered him with questions about his future, quizzing him on his plans after basketball. The conversations often ended in arguments followed by silence. Patricia worried about Lenny. Basketball had consumed his life since childhood, and without it, he seemed adrift.

He pulled out his phone, opened Instagram, and noticed a message from Tim. It was a clip of Stephon in Tall Trees. Lenny replayed the clip again. Stephon had talent. There was something so raw and natural about his game. He had so much room for improvement.

"There you are," Eddie said in his booming voice as he closed the door to the house and walked toward Lenny.

Lenny put his phone away. "Hey," he replied.

"Hay is for horses." Eddie walked up to Lenny, hands dug in his pockets. "Something my father used to say. We all turn into our parents one day."

Lenny chuckled awkwardly. "I guess."

"I want to talk to you."

"About?"

"Your momma is worried about you." Eddie pulled out a pack of cigarettes and tapped it against his hand, then extracted one. "You mind?" Lenny shook his head. "Bad habit, I know. But what's a man without his vices?" Eddie lit his cigarette. "Your Momma, she's worried."

"I know. Worrying about me is her part-time job."

"You might be right. You know her better than I do."

"Yeah, I do."

Eddie nodded and looked up at the sky. "Beautiful night, huh?"

"Yeah, it is."

"When I retired, I was lost. I joined the force right after I graduated from high school. Law enforcement was my life, my purpose. Once I no longer had to put on the blue, I didn't feel like the same person. I felt like I lost my purpose. You not putting on that basketball uniform anymore, I know how you feel."

"My career might not be over."

"But," Eddie finished the cigarette and stomped it out on the ground, "it might be. And what are you going to do next? Are you prepared for that?"

"I'll figure it out."

"Not in a bottle you won't. You drank half a bottle of wine like it was water, Son."

"I had a few glasses over dinner; I'm good."

"But we both know it's not just wine over dinner. We know it's more than that."

"Look, Eddie, I hear what you're saying, and I know my mom likes you, but you don't know me."

Eddie pulled out his wallet and removed a sobriety coin. He held it up for Lenny to see. "Twenty years sober. I know you because I was you." Eddie picked up the cigarette butt, blew it off, and stuck it in the back pocket of his jeans. "Don't tell your Momma about the cigarettes. She thinks I quit."

Eddie walked to the driver's side of a newer model Chevy Silverado and slid into the driver's seat. Lenny began walking back to the house. "Hold up. I got something for you."

Lenny exhaled deeply and turned around. Eddie waved him over. Lenny walked to the driver's side window. Eddie placed a book in Lenny's hand: Poems by William Ernest Henley.

"A book of poetry?" Lenny asked with a hint of contempt.

"I am the master of my fate; I am the captain of my soul," Eddie responded. "Poetry saved my life." Eddie turned the key in the ignition and shifted the truck into reverse.

CHAPTER 9

Sacrifice for the Team

Overseas, Lenny looked forward to Saturday mornings. They were reserved for his ritual 6-mile run. When he lived in Europe, he jogged through the parks near his apartment while listening to 8Ball and MJG, Playa Fly, 3-6 Mafia, and other legendary Memphis artists. The songs transported him back home when he needed it most. He could lose himself in his playlist and run for hours—no anxiety about practice, games, or making the NBA; just one foot in front of the other and the path ahead.

Now that he was back home, his discipline wavered. Late Friday nights at Sunnybrook made early Saturday mornings almost unbearable. He found himself doing more drinking than jogging.

Lenny lay in his bed unconscious. Sunrise slowly brought light into his room. An annoying chime blasted from his phone at 6:00 a.m. He rolled over toward the nightstand and slapped the screen like he was killing a mosquito. Silence for a few seconds. Then he heard the creaking sound of his bedroom door opening.

"Lenny," Patricia whispered. "You sleep?"

"I was, Ma," Lenny responded, slightly annoyed.

"There's someone here to see you," Patricia said mysteriously.

"What?" Lenny replied, confused and groggy. "Mane, tell Jamel it's too early…"

Before he could finish, Tim pushed open the door and peeked in.

"Tim?" Lenny asked incredulously.

"I'll leave you two alone," Patricia said with a smile at Lenny as she walked away.

Lenny sat up, shirtless, with his back resting against the cold wooden headboard. Blankets covered him from the waist down. He wiped his eyes. Tim walked to the far side of the room, where a dated dresser and mirror set rested against a window.

"Been at least 15 years since I've been in this room," Tim broke the silence while staring into the mirror.

"Remember, you, me, and Jamel got dressed for prom right here?" Tim chuckled while pointing near the dresser. "Took us forever to fix our cufflinks."

The memory made Lenny smile. "No YouTube back then. Trial and error," he remembered.

Tim took a seat in a dingy recliner chair near the dresser. He glanced at a half-empty bottle of Remy next to his foot. The smell of alcohol and body odor permeated the room.

"Don't remember you being much of a morning person," Lenny told Tim, trying to figure out why he was there.

"I ain't got no choice. Got kids to feed now," Tim said, noticing Lenny's hangover-ridden face. "To keep it 100, your mom told me to stop by. Says you've been hitting Sunnybrook every night. Letting yourself go." Tim paused and cut his eyes in Lenny's direction. "You alright, bro?"

"I'm good, fam," Lenny muttered, letting out a belch. "Moms is always overreacting, you know that. I just had a tryout with the Celtics, bro. I'm good."

Tim looked skeptical. "Oh yeah? How'd that go?" he asked with a hint of sarcasm.

Lenny scratched his head.

"On the real, did you have time to think about our conversation at Sunnybrook…?" Tim interjected.

Before Tim could finish his sentence, his iPhone FaceTime notification began chiming. He accepted the call. Lenny looked annoyed.

"Principal Davenport. To what do I owe this pleasure on a Saturday morning?" Tim answered, holding his phone up to his face.

Lenny tensed up and remained quiet. He couldn't believe Tim answered the phone. He hadn't heard Katrina's voice in years. Her familiar heavy, southern accent brought back a rush of memories.

"Tim, fall conditioning starts next week, and we don't have a head coach. Where are we with that?" Principal Davenport asked impatiently.

"Where are you, anyway?" she continued. "That place looks familiar."

Lenny waved his arms in distress, pleading for Tim not to reveal his location. Tim smiled.

"Perfect timing," Tim said, grinning. "I'm interviewing one of the candidates right now."

Lenny cursed under his breath and threw a pillow at Tim. Tim reversed the camera on his screen and pointed it at Lenny. An awkward silence followed.

"Lenny Chase?" she blurted out, shocked.

Lenny rubbed his head nervously. "In the flesh," he responded, trying to hide his embarrassment.

"I didn't know you were coaching now. Hell, I didn't know you were back in Memphis."

Tim recognized Lenny's discomfort, turned the camera back, and spoke for him. "Still ballin' overseas, but I'm trying to get the superstar to stay home and help out his alma mater. Coach Heard would be proud." Tim glanced at Lenny. "Ain't that right, Lenny?"

Lenny flashed Tim the middle finger.

Principal Davenport sensed Tim's attempted deflection. "Well, if things don't work out, I'd love...we'd love to have you back at MLK. These kids need you."

Tim and Lenny locked eyes and exchanged smiles. Lenny's confidence returned.

"Thanks, Trina. I'll think about it," Lenny responded.

"It's Principal Davenport," she corrected him. "Tim, call me later."

Tim ended the call and avoided eye contact with Lenny. "You didn't have to put me on blast like that, bro."

Tim didn't respond. He grabbed the bottle of Remy from the floor, raised up from his seat, and walked toward the door with it. "Coach Heard used to say, 'Sacrifice for the team, and the rest will take care of itself.'" Tim stopped before leaving the room. "Let me know what you decide."

The door shut behind Tim. Lenny exhaled deeply, his chest heavy. Both Tim and Principal Davenport's words left a gnawing sense of duty swirling in the pit of his stomach. Coach Heard's voice echoed in his head: "Sacrifice for the team." He could still see Coach Heard pacing the sidelines, hands on his hips, staring him down during those final drills. "When you give your best, the rest takes care of itself," the old man had told him before the state championship. It wasn't about winning; it was about showing up.

Lenny picked up his phone and opened a text thread with AJ. His thumb hovered over the keys as doubt crept in. What if this was another mistake? He swallowed the thought, typed the message *AJ, I think I'm done*, but before he could hit send, three dots began to dance in the thread. A message from AJ appeared:

A.J.: Yo Lenny, I might have an opportunity for you overseas. Let's talk at the gym later today.

Lenny tossed the phone onto the nightstand and slumped back against the headboard. As he stared at the cracks in the ceiling, he thought about Coach Heard again. The cracks weren't flaws; they were proof the house still stood. He jumped out of bed, put on his running clothes, laced up his shoes, and dashed out of the house.

CHAPTER 10

Father Time

Lenny parked his car at East High School and reached across his seat to snatch his gym bag from the passenger side. He hopped out of his car wearing Nike slides, gym shorts, and a dry-fit tank top and headed toward the school gym.

On Saturday afternoons, A.J. organized a closed gym for his current and potential clients in the Memphis area. He made sure the runs were exclusive and not open to the public to protect them from the violence that often erupted during Memphis pickup games. He even hired his own security for the closed sessions to ensure anyone not invited was turned away.

When Lenny made his way to the gym door, a 6'5" muscular white man with a bald head and chest-length scruffy beard greeted him. A gun was nestled in a holster on his waist. The guard recognized Lenny from previous closed sessions and simply nodded toward the gym without speaking.

Inside the gym, you could hear balls bouncing on hardwood, rims vibrating from players dunking, and nets swishing. The gym had a mix of players on the court from high school, collegiate, and professional levels. A.J. was well connected. A.J. approached Lenny, and they greeted each other with pound hugs.

"So, what's this opportunity, bro?" Lenny asked with arms folded. "I'm not going back to Montenegro again and playing for peanuts."

A.J. shrugged his shoulders. "Hey, a job is a job," he responded flatly. "Look, Armani Milan is looking for a shooting guard. They had a rep at your Celtics workout and want to fly you out next week."

"You serious?!" Lenny exclaimed, grinning from ear to ear. "They paid my boy Jason 1.5 million for one season, and I averaged way more than him." Lenny hugged A.J.

A.J. patted him lightly on the back, feeling slightly awkward about Lenny's premature reaction. "Calm down. Nothing is set in stone yet. Now get this run started; I got a date with your mom later," A.J. joked.

Lenny laced up his Kobe Retro 6s and walked onto the court with a newfound swagger. Teams were quickly selected, and the session began. A.J. watched from the sidelines while talking on the phone with an SEC coach. A small group of players sprawled out around the gym, waiting for their turn.

Lenny dribbled the ball up the court and was greeted at half court by a 6'2" high school player named Michael. Michael was only 17, but he was 195 pounds and played like a grown man. He was fearless and did not back down from Lenny. Michael was in a defensive stance with his forearm resting on Lenny's waist, reaching for the ball. Lenny used his body to keep the high schooler at bay while surveying the court and mapping out his next move.

"I got one!" Lenny shouted to his team. "Clear out. This a bucket!" He waved off his teammates.

"Ain't gonna be easy, ole head," Michael whispered to Lenny.

Lenny flashed a grin and swatted Michael's hand away with his off arm. Then he exploded—shoulder down, pure acceleration—

leaving Michael scrambling in his wake. Michael recovered fast, but Lenny was already spinning left, turning his defender into a statue at the three-point line.

The lane opened like the Red Sea. Lenny rose, cocking the ball back with both hands, ready to demolish the rim. For a split second, he hung in the air like he owned gravity itself.

Then everything went wrong.

He released the rim too early, legs unprepared for the fall. His body hit the hardwood with a sickening *crack* that cut through the gym like a gunshot. Lenny's scream tore from somewhere deep, raw and primal. Silence swallowed the gym whole. Even A.J. hung up his phone.

URGENT CARE

Lenny and A.J. sat in one of the rooms at Memphis Urgent Center, awaiting the doctor's return with X-rays. Lenny grimaced in pain each time he tried to step down from the adjustable medical table.

"This is nothing. I've dealt with worse before," Lenny tried to convince A.J., and himself.

A.J. continued staring down at his text messages. Armani Milan's coach wanted to sign Lenny. They had salary space for a two-year, $3.5 million contract. The coach was awaiting A.J.'s response. He didn't want to tell Lenny. Not yet.

"Damn bruh, say something," Lenny complained. "Don't just sit there."

As Lenny spoke, the door swung open and Dr. Walker strolled in with the nurse who had taken Lenny's vitals. Dr. Walker was a 65-year-old African American man with mahogany brown skin, wearing reading glasses and a white lab coat. He had a clipboard in his hand with X-ray files. When he entered, Lenny sat up on the edge of the table, and A.J. put his phone away.

"Give it to me straight, doc. Don't sugarcoat it," Lenny begged.

"No need to worry; you'll be fine. You're relatively young, so you'll bounce back in no time," Dr. Walker promised Lenny. "I'm going to prescribe some painkillers, put you in a boot for a few weeks and refer you to an orthopedic doctor."

Lenny began to smile in A.J.'s direction; A.J. did not smile back. He had been in too many of these visits with players to share Lenny's premature excitement. Instead, he turned to Dr. Walker.

"What are Lenny's chances of playing professional basketball again, Dr.?" A.J. asked.

Dr. Walker's eyebrows raised in confusion. "Professional basketball?" He looked at Lenny with bewilderment. "Oh no, son. You will walk again, maybe run, but your playing days are over. You have no cartilage left in your knee."

"What about surgery?" A.J. asked.

"Chances are slim that surgery will help. He's young, but not *that* young," Dr. Walker explained.

Dr. Walker placed the clipboard under his armpit and gave Lenny a sympathetic look. "This happens to the best of them. Father time is undefeated."

Lenny was frozen stiff. The news landed like a death sentence as he stared at the walls looking dejected.

"I'll give you two some time," Dr. Walker stated as he and the nurse walked out of the room.

A.J. got up from his chair and rested his hand on Lenny's shoulder. "I'm sorry, man."

CHAPTER 11

Card Declined

Lenny pulled his Challenger into a tight parking space in front of Shoprite Liquors. Lenny's cousin, Jamel, was riding shotgun, holding his phone up to his mouth, arguing with one of his baby mothers about late child support payments.

Neon beer signs on the barred windows flicked to life as dusk descended on Orange Mound. Gang graffiti covered almost every inch of the brick building. A giant "We Accept EBT" sign hung above the door. Jamel hopped out first. He sat on the hood of the car and continued to argue. When Lenny got out, Jamel paused his conversation. "Lemme get some hot fries, bruh!" Lenny nodded.

MEMPHIS 1988

Shoprite was a staple in the neighborhood. The store opened in the early 1970s by Dave and Linda Ali. Back then, Kimball Avenue was thriving with Black-owned businesses. You had Jackson Groceries, where all the Black people went for produce and meat. Friendlies was where folks stopped for ice cream and pastries. And Cavalier, a men's clothing store that sold made-to-measure shirts and custom suits.

Linda Ali inherited farmland in Bartlett, Tennessee, an area just thirty minutes outside Memphis. The young couple was in their early 30s. They sold their farmland, moved to Memphis, and opened their first business, Shoprite Liquors.

In the early 1980s, crack cocaine flooded cities across America, and Memphis was no exception. Violence and murder ruined families and ravaged neighborhoods. Orange Mound, the country's second Black neighborhood, was hit especially hard.

On a cold fall Monday night in 1988, a week before Thanksgiving, Linda stood behind the cash register, flipping through a Jet magazine. Dave was in the store's basement working on an inventory list for the upcoming holiday and watching Monday Night Football on a small black-and-white television.

Dave and Linda ran Shoprite with only one other employee, Terrell, a failed musician and occasional heroin user. He had been missing more and more time from work, claiming sickness as an excuse. Over breakfast that morning, Dave and Linda had discussed the need to find a new employee. Terrell had become unreliable, and the demands of the store were beginning to be too much for just two people.

It had been a slow night, typical for a Monday. A little after 8:00 p.m., a masked gunman entered Shoprite with a black handgun. Linda froze at the sight of the gun pointed in her direction. She dropped the magazine.

"Give me the money, bitch," the gunman demanded.

She recognized the voice right away. "Terrell?" she asked.

Dave heard the rapid gunfire. He froze, then leapt into action, armed only with a box cutter he used to open beer cases. Upstairs, he found the store empty and his wife dead, shot in the face. The cash register was gone.

Police found Terrell a few days later in an abandoned car. The cash register was in the trunk. He had overdosed. Dave sold Shoprite a few months later to an Iranian man who owned multiple liquor stores and cash-checking businesses throughout Memphis.

PRESENT DAY

The door chimed as Lenny entered Shoprite, dragging his foot in a boot. A burly armed security guard sat in a metal folding chair, hand on his gun. He glanced at Lenny with disinterest before going back to scrolling through his phone. The store was lit with blinding bright white lights. Lenny adjusted his eyes. Moneybagg Yo's "Time Today" blasted from the store's ceiling speakers.

Lenny made his way through a corridor of snacks, grabbed a bag of hot fries, and proceeded to the counter where a skinny Iranian American teenager stood behind bulletproof security glass. He was dressed in G-Star Raw jeans and a G-Star Raw t-shirt. He spoke Farsi into a Bluetooth headset. He greeted Lenny with a head nod but didn't end his phone conversation.

"Remy VSOP," Lenny hollered over the loud music.

The teenager didn't acknowledge Lenny, but he walked a few steps to where the cognacs were shelved and grabbed a Remy box. He dusted it off with a paper towel and punched a button on the cash register. The tiny screen read 34.99 in digital numbers. Lenny slid his credit card into the spinning transaction window. The teenager removed the headset.

"Bruh, card declined."

"Run it again."

The teenager ran it again. He slid the card back to Lenny.

"Declined." The teenager shrugged.

"Shit." Lenny took his card back, opened his wallet, and removed a twenty-dollar bill—his last bit of cash. "What can I get for twenty?"

CHAPTER 12

The Queen

Principal Davenport was pedaling feverishly on a Peloton bike in the basement of her spacious home. She lived in an affluent community in South Memphis that young Black professionals called the Hill. In this half-mile block resided a cluster of doctors, lawyers, politicians, and businesspeople with connections, money, and influence. Principal Davenport moved there when she accepted the job at MLK; it reminded her of her time in D.C. at Howard University, surrounded by affluent Black people making power moves.

A digital window on her Peloton bike's screen showed a video chat with Stacy, one of her sorority line sisters from Howard. On Saturdays, the two shared stories while logging miles on their bikes.

"I just can't find a decent man out here, Stacy," Principal Davenport complained while out of breath. "Your husband know any good guys?"

"Girl listen, the grass isn't always greener. My husband makes good money, but he ain't never home. Kids barely know him. The Amazon delivery guy steps on that front porch more than he does," Stacy responded.

"Be careful with that," Principal Davenport warned. "My ex-husband was always traveling on business too. You see how that ended up."

"Hey, I've already done the math. Five more years and his 401(k) vests. Then he can leave if he wants; hell, just give me my half."

Principal Davenport burst out laughing at the screen. "Girl, you're crazy." The two began to pedal slower as their workout came to an end. "I did see Lenny Chase the other day."

"Wait. Is this the high school crush that got away?" Stacy asked excitedly.

"More like ran away," Principal Davenport scoffed. "He always loved basketball more than anything else."

"Girl, that's men for you. Chasing dreams while running away from responsibility."

"I offered him the coaching job at MLK. We need a coach, and I can't think of anyone more passionate about the game." Principal Davenport jumped off her bike and dried her face with a towel. "We'll see if he takes it."

"Are you sure it's just the job you're hoping he's still passionate about?" Stacy responded with a smirk.

"Girl, bye." Principal Davenport waved and clicked off the screen.

The warm shower and breakfast felt like armor, preparing her for what came next. Principal Davenport stood in front of her bedroom closet, staring up at the purple shoebox that had been collecting dust on the top shelf for years. Her hands trembled slightly as she pulled it down. She sank onto the bed's edge, the box heavy with more than just memories. The lid came off with a soft *pop*, releasing the faint scent of old paper and time. Her breath caught.

High school photos smiled back at her—a girl she barely recognized with bright eyes and endless possibilities. Yellowed newspaper clippings chronicled her track victories in faded ink. A small diary with a broken clasp. Her parents together in happier times, before the lawyers and the silence. And at the bottom, an old VHS tape marked *Track Meets* in her teenage handwriting.

She picked up the tape, its plastic case worn smooth from handling, and wondered if she still had the courage to press play.

Principal Davenport pulled out the diary and used a rusty key from the bottom of the shoe box to open it. She flipped through the pages, and a withered letter fell out. She read it to herself.

The Queen

Since the first day we met
I knew it was true
That no matter how old we get
I would never leave you
The feelings we share
Are hard to describe
Whenever you're here
I feel more alive
If it wasn't for you
I don't know where I'd be
One thing is true
You are forever my Queen
~ Lenny

Principal Davenport smiled and placed the letter back into the box.

CHAPTER 13

The King

Jamel sat down next to Lenny on a sagging park bench facing the outdoor basketball court at Gaston Community Center. The sun was setting on a breezy Memphis night. Renovations prevented them from going inside. A half-empty bottle of Remy sat between the two.

"On my momma, this junt getting on my nerves," Jamel complained. He stuffed his phone deep into his jeans pocket. He exhaled and drank from a red Dixie cup. Lenny just laughed and sipped from an identical cup.

On the court, a group of middle school-aged boys played a sloppy game of pickup basketball. They all lacked fundamentals. It was riddled with over-dribbling, poor shooting, half-effort defense, and picky foul calls.

"Aye, remember when this was the spot?" Jamel said. "If you lost, it'd be hours before you got back on. We had some fire runs down here."

Lenny nodded. The courts at Gaston Community Center are hallowed ground among street-ballers. Players from all over Memphis knew to bring their A-game. The list of Memphis greats who cut their teeth at GCC is long and distinguished.

"You okay, man?" Jamel asked. "You've been quiet all day. You depressed or something?"

"I saw Trina the other day."

Jamel hopped off the bench, spilling some of his drink. He stood in front of Lenny. "You talking about Trina, Trina?!" Jamel stared intently.

"Yes, fool." Lenny rolled his eyes.

"And where was this?" Jamel asked, palms up.

"FaceTime. Tim, crazy ass, was at the house."

"I know she's still fine. Wait, why is she FaceTiming you anyway?"

"She wants me to be head coach."

Jamel threw his hands up in the air. His cup went flying. He jumped up and down excitedly. "For real? You lying, bruh?"

"On everything I love." Lenny took another sip.

Jamel grinned. "You gotta take that job."

"I don't know, man. I still wanna hoop."

Jamel sat back down. He took Lenny's cup, drank from it, and stared off into the distance.

"Be happy you had a career. You traveled the world, bro. Played ball for a living." Jamel pointed to a group of young boys. "Those kids ain't leaving Memphis, ever. Neither am I." The two shared a moment of silence.

"Remember what Coach Heard always said?" Jamel puffed his chest out and put his hands on his hips. "I'm not teaching you the fundamentals of basketball, son; I'm teaching you the fundamentals of life," he enunciated in a baritone voice.

They both burst out laughing, lightening the mood.

Jamel stopped laughing. His voice cracked. "But real talk, if it wasn't for Coach H, I'd probably be in the pen with my Pops right now." As Jamel spoke, an argument broke out among the teens. Jamel yelled at the group to go home, and they dispersed.

Jamel took the last sip of Remy from the cup. He pulled up his sleeve and pointed to a dated tattoo of a bulldog on his shoulder. "Remember when we got those tattoos together after winning state?" Jamel asked.

Lenny pulled up his sleeve and revealed a tattoo with the words "King of Memphis" arched over his shoulder.

Jamel poked Lenny's tattoo. "Don't ever forget that, bruh."

CHAPTER 14

Me and You

L enny stumbled through his bedroom door, the world still spinning from too many drinks with Jamel at Gaston. His legs gave out, depositing him hard on the carpet beside his bed. The high school yearbook sat there like it had been waiting—spine cracked, pages worn from too many late-night visits.

He flipped through memories until he found it: the superlatives' page. There they were, frozen in time under "Most Athletic"—him in his MLK jersey, basketball cradled against his hip like a promise he couldn't keep, and Principal Davenport in her black tracksuit, gold winged foot blazing across her chest, caught mid-sprint toward a future that actually happened.

We need you. Her words echoed in his skull, sharp and persistent even through the alcohol fog.

He dragged himself to the desk, laptop screen glowing like a beacon. His fingers found the familiar search—Cassie's "Me & U," the same song that used to pump him up before games, back when everything seemed possible. The melody drifted through cheap speakers as his eyelids grew heavy.

Sleep pulled him under, carrying him into dreams where he was still seventeen and the world still believed in him.

2006

It was the fall of 2006. Lenny and Katrina, both 17 years old, were inside Lenny's bedroom. Outside, the rain was falling in sheets. Music played softly from a radio.

Lenny was lying on the floor, facing the ceiling. He spun a basketball on his fingertips. He wore basketball shorts and a T-shirt with the University of Maryland's Terrapin logo. Trina sat on the bed, legs crossed, finishing homework. She was dressed in an MLK tracksuit.

Lenny stopped spinning the ball. He palmed it and held it up in the air. "I hate when it rains. Can't get any shots in."

"You could do your homework."

Lenny chuckled. "That's why I got you!"

"You ought to be banned for wearing those shorts in this city. You know it's Tiger Nation with me." Trina responded as she threw a pillow at Lenny. It hit him on the head, and he dropped the ball.

"Hey," he shrieked. Lenny turned over, pushed himself up, and rested on his elbows. "You almost done?"

Trina closed her textbook. "What are you going to do next year in college?" Trina asked. "It's student-athlete, not athlete-student. Ball players still have to do homework."

Lenny climbed onto the bed. He pulled Trina close to him. They kissed. "You'll be at Howard; I'll be at Maryland. Close enough for you to still do my homework!"

Trina playfully pushed Lenny away. "Lenny Chase has all the answers."

"Yep."

"You sure you're not going to want those Maryland groupies to help you with your homework?"

Lenny sucked his teeth. "There you go! You know I ain't into groupies. You're all the groupie I need."

"Whatever!" Trina yelled while grabbing another pillow from the bed and pummeling Lenny.

"Just me," Trina whispered. Lenny nodded, and Trina kissed him. "Better be just me." They kissed again. Trina perked up. "It's our song."

"Our song?" Lenny asked skeptically.

"Yesss." Trina hopped off the bed and turned the volume up on the radio. Cassie's "Me & U" was playing. She swayed her hips to the music. "Every couple has a song. This is ours."

CHAPTER 15

One More Night

Stephon awoke to the yells of guards shouting. His eyes quickly adjusted to the thin rays of sunshine that broke through a small rectangular window in the back of his cell.

The stone walls of the cell were covered with crudely etched gang symbols and the nicknames of former juveniles. The silver combination toilet and sink that was loosely attached to the wall dripped. The smell of urine, body odor, and sewage was an overwhelming presence.

"Rise and shine, boys; it's almost breakfast time," barked Troy, a 36-year-old Black C.O. who dragged his aluminum baton across the bars of the cell. Troy was built like a gorilla and had a reputation for excessive force. The juveniles hated him.

Stephon sat up in bed. He wiped the sleep from his eyes and yawned. "D-Lo, you up?"

Stephon heard no answer. Confused, he dropped down from his bunk and observed an empty bunk bed below.

"Open cell number 8," barked Dan, a white middle-aged C.O. with a walrus mustache.

Stephon backed away from the cell door as it opened to Dan standing behind a seventeen-year-old nicknamed Smoke. Teardrops were tattooed under his brown eyes, and he sported a mohawk. He stood 6'3" with a lanky, athletic build, and his forearms were branded with two Fs, a symbol of affiliation with the Frayser Fiends.

Dan shoved Smoke into the cell.

"Chill, my nigga," Smoke said without turning around.

"You chill, *my nigga*," Dan replied with a grin. "D-Lo turned eighteen last night, graduated to the big leagues. Meet your new roommate. You boys best get along. Thirty minutes 'til breakfast; have your asses ready."

Stephon kept quiet as the door shut behind Dan's remarks. Smoke's eyes surveyed the entire cell before they stopped on Stephon, making eye contact for the first time.

"I don't sleep on bottom," said Smoke.

Smoke cracked his knuckles as he spoke. Stephon remembered D-Lo's warning about not making enemies.

"Top bunk is taken, fam," responded Stephon. He folded his arms across his chest.

A condescending smirk flashed across Smoke's face as he began placing his belongings on Stephon's bunk without speaking. Stephon's blood boiled. His heart pounded inside his chest.

"My nigga, you got the world fucked up," screamed Stephon as he rushed his new cellmate.

Stephon speared Smoke with his shoulder, ramming him in the chest. They both crashed into the bottom bunk. Stephon delivered wild punches to Smoke's head. Chants of "fight, fight, fight" erupted from the surrounding cells.

The cell door swung open, and Dan and another Black C.O. named Rick rushed into the room. They separated the two, slammed them to the ground, and pressed both of their faces into the floor. Stephon continued to resist.

"I see you two have the hots for each other already. A few hours in the hole should cool you off a bit," Dan shouted.

Rick escorted Stephon out the door in cuffs. His half-shut, blackened eye menaced in Smoke's direction. Three words fell softly from Smoke's bloody lips as he smiled.

"You dead, nigga."

Stephon sat on the floor of a windowless cell. Darkness surrounded him. Despair engulfed him. He could hear the groans of fellow inmates outside in the yard, suffering from the unbearable Memphis heat. Sweat dripped from his face into his lap as he watched a four-legged creature scurry across the floor of his cell. Stephon hated rats, but his thoughts were so consumed by the grim outlook of his future at Tall Trees that he ignored the rodent. His scuffle with Smoke earned him beef with the Frayser Fiends, and word surely had spread among the juveniles. It was only a matter of time before they retaliated.

"Open cell twelve!" ordered a guard.

Stephon's heart began to race as his cell door slowly opened. Returning to general population was suicide at this point. A portly guard entered; his hand gripped the handle of a baton.

"Where y'all taking me?" Stephon asked.

"Shut up and walk with me," the C.O. demanded.

Stephon walked past a row of cells with young men's hands grasping the bars, peering into the corridor.

"That's yo ass when you get back on the yard," remarked a heavyset sixteen-year-old with a mini-afro and dark-brown skin. His cheek displayed a green tattoo of two Fs overlapping.

The guard took Stephon into an empty conference room with white walls and round tables. He uncuffed Stephon and left the room. A loud buzzer sounded—the sound of an electronic door opening. Stephon's city-appointed attorney, David Miller, entered the conference room.

David was middle-aged and balding. He wore a black polyester suit and carried a battered briefcase. "My name is David Miller; I'm your attorney." David extended his hand. Stephon clumsily shook it. "Please, have a seat," David suggested as he pointed in the direction of a table in the middle of the room.

"What took you so long?" Stephon responded. He snatched up a chair from the other side of the table and plopped down with his arms folded.

"What happened to your eye?" David responded with a look of concern, staring at the purple bruise surrounding Stephon's right cheek.

"Look, I need you to get me out of here," Stephon demanded while simultaneously pressing his finger into the table. "Today."

"Let's discuss your case." David removed a file folder and legal pad from his briefcase. "The police affidavit says a gun was found in your locker. Did you say anything before they arrested you?"

"Naw."

"Good. Does anyone else have access to your locker? Did you ever give anyone else the code? Leave your locker open?"

Stephon put his head in his hands, becoming frustrated with the questioning. "Man, where are my sisters at? They're supposed to have seen me by now," Stephon responded.

David put down his pen and closed his notepad. He stood up from the table and went to the other side where Stephon sat, placing his arm around his shoulder. "Listen, I know you're scared, son. But you're strong. I'm going to get you through this, and I promise I'll get you out of here."

Stephon's eyes began to water as tears fell onto his legs, creating dark spots on his orange jumpsuit.

"Today is Saturday. Your hearing is Monday. Judge Wilson."

A loud buzzer interrupted David's words as Troy entered the conference room. "Time's up!" Troy barked. "Let's go."

Troy snapped the cuffs tightly around Stephon's wrists, causing obvious discomfort.

"Hey! There's no need for all that!" David yelled as he stood up from the table, watching Troy usher Stephon away.

Stephon looked back and spoke. "Monday?! I won't last one more night in this place."

CHAPTER 16

Think Before You Move

A few hours after Stephon's meeting with David, Troy grabbed him again from his solitary cell and led him into a small, lifeless room. Sadat sat at a table, grasping a cup of steaming tea. He was in his mid-fifties, thin, dark-skinned, with a bald head and a perfectly trimmed beard. He wore a thobe over black jeans and black Timberland boots. A beat-up chess set sat on the table.

Stephon looked at Sadat and then at Troy.

"Sit, nigga," Troy barked. He shoved Stephon toward the table, puffed out his chest, and exited the room.

Stephon looked Sadat up and down, his icy gaze fixed on him. Sadat put his cigarette out on the table.

"No need for the stare down, son," Sadat calmly explained. "I'm not one of those guards."

Stephon took a seat, still unsure if he could trust Sadat. "Who are you?"

"Sadat. Rehab specialist. For your case."

"What kind of name is that?"

"It's Arabic. It means gentleman."

"You Muslim?"

"Five percent nation."

Stephon's defensiveness softened. "My dad was Muslim," he said, finally looking Sadat in the eye. "What do you want?"

"It's about what you want. Do you want to stay in here or go home?"

"Go home," Stephon quickly replied.

"Well, that's where I come in. See, the state of Tennessee pays me a pitiful salary to determine whether young men like you stay in a youth center or jail, or whether they can be rehabilitated."

"So, what do I have to do?"

"Talk. Answer my questions. Stay out of trouble too. Fighting doesn't help your situation."

"And if I don't talk, then what?"

"Then you stay here or get moved to a youth center."

"Fine. Let's get this over with."

"Good." Sadat leaned back in his chair. "What are you scared of?"

"Nothing," Stephon snarled.

"Then why'd you bring a gun to school?" Sadat coolly asked.

Stephon hesitated.

Sadat interrupted the silence. "I've been doing this for a while, son; snitching isn't part of the job."

"Would you believe me if I told you it wasn't mine?" Stephon asked, giving a sidelong glance.

Sadat rubbed his chin. "I looked through your file. No visitors. Where's your mom? Dad? Girlfriend? Or boyfriend?"

Stephon laughed. "I'm not gay, bro."

Sadat raised his hands, palms up, in peace. "No disrespect."

Stephon paced the room. "My oldest sister is gay. I don't know where my mom is. My dad is dead."

"Hard growing up with no father. I've been there. My dad was a rolling stone too. Here today, gone tomorrow. I have more half-brothers and sisters in Memphis than I'll ever meet."

"My pops wasn't like that. He was around. Car accident."

"Well, my dad wasn't worth much, but he did one good thing for me."

Stephon gestured inquisitively with a shrug.

"He taught me chess." Sadat opened the chess set. "You play?"

Stephon shook his head no.

"Want to learn?"

Stephon shrugged. "If it gets me out of here, why not?"

Sadat began setting up the chessboard. "So, no mother or father. Who do you live with now?"

"My grandmother and two sisters."

"Grandmothers are a blessing. I miss my Nana." Sadat finished arranging the chess pieces. "I love chess because it teaches you about life."

"How?" Stephon asked, staring at the chess pieces.

"Life is one big chessboard," Sadat replied. "We are the pieces. In chess and in life, every decision has an impact. One bad move — and it's game over or it's hard to recover from."

Stephon sat quietly, taking it all in.

"They say you can hoop," Sadat switched topics. "Guards said they made a lot of money off you Friday."

"I'm done with basketball," Stephon said with an empty stare. "I just needed to get my mind off this place."

Sadat leaned back in his chair, rubbing his hands together. "Let's play another game then." Sadat pointed to the chessboard.

Stephon exhaled deeply and folded his arms across his chest. "Alright, man."

Sadat rubbed his chin and nodded in acknowledgment. "In chess—and in life—you must think before you move."

CHAPTER 17

Last Shot

A week after Stephon visited solitary, Judge Wilson entered the small conference room outside his chambers, carrying a stack of manila folders. He gingerly sat down at the head of the long conference table. He was in his early seventies, with neatly combed white hair and a freshly shaven face. He walked with a slight limp, favoring his left leg. He was bothered by arthritis induced by years of wear and tear on the hardwood.

During his youth in Bowling Green, Kentucky, Judge Wilson scoured the city for pickup games. He cared less about segregation and often found himself playing hoops in Black neighborhoods. It was more competitive. His uncanny jumping ability for a white kid earned him the nickname "Bunny" and later secured him a scholarship to play for legendary coach Adolph Rupp at the University of Kentucky.

Judge Wilson was a backup guard on the Wildcats team that played in the historic 1966 NCAA championship game against Texas Western (now UTEP), which marked the first contest between an all-white starting five (Kentucky) and an all-black starting five (Texas Western) in the NCAA championship game.

After two decades as a prominent defense attorney, Judge Wilson chose to finish his legal career on the bench. He was one of the few white judges in Memphis known for showing compassion for Black youth. He favored diversion and "first offender" programs.

His chamber walls were covered in wooden panels with bookshelves embedded inside. Hundreds of red and green-spined books with gold trim were tucked tightly into the shelves surrounding the conference table. Wood-framed portraits of snow-haired white men in robes hung in a semi-circle along the walls.

Principal Davenport sat at the opposite end of the conference table, next to Stephon's public defender, David Miller. Across from them sat Assistant District Attorney Rebecca Tanner.

Judge Wilson looked over the assembled group. "Okay, folks. Why are we here today? Let's make it quick; I have a ton of arraignments this morning that I'm not looking forward to."

"Your Honor, the defense is seeking special treatment because the defendant is a star basketball player," Rebecca said. "The fact of the matter is he had a gun in his locker, and he should be prosecuted just like everyone else. No special treatment for athletes."

Ms. Davenport shot Rebecca a look of disdain. Rebecca avoided eye contact.

"Your Honor, this is my client's first contact with the criminal justice system," David piped in. "My client is like a lot of young men you see in this courthouse every day. He comes from a troubled background. His father was killed in a car accident a few months ago. His mother is in prison. His elderly grandmother is raising him in South Memphis."

"Your Honor, Stephon is a good kid," Ms. Davenport said. "He has a chance to be just the second person in his family to attend college, something that very few of our students get the chance to do at MLK."

Rebecca gave a disapproving gesture. "Your Honor, Ms. Davenport is the one who called the police in the first place."

"Judge, there's no need to hold this young man any longer. He's not a danger to the community." David changed topics.

Judge Wilson nodded. "What are you asking?"

"My ask, our ask, is that if you release him pending resolution of this case. This will give Stephon the opportunity to return to school and finish his junior year."

"Your Honor, this is absurd," Rebecca interjected, her voice raised. "The gun was recovered from the defendant's locker—his locker. Now they want him back in school?"

Judge Wilson nodded solemnly. He looked over at David and Principal Davenport. "Mr. Miller and Ms. Davenport, it sounds like you're asking me to ignore the law for your client."

"No, Your Honor, we are not asking you to ignore the law. We are asking for this young man to get an opportunity to finish the school year, maybe even attend college one day," David noted.

Rebecca huffed dismissively.

Judge Wilson slowly and silently flipped through Stephon's file.

David and Principal Davenport, sat quietly, awaiting a response. Principal Davenport nervously tapped her fingers on the table.

Judge Wilson looked up from the file. "His file says his father was Camron Johnson. Is that Cam Johnson of the Memphis Lords?"

Rebecca nodded affirmatively. "That's him, Your Honor. He did five years at West Tennessee Detention for armed robbery," she said.

Judge Wilson addressed Rebecca directly. "I know, Counselor; I was the one who sentenced him."

"Mr. Johnson served his time and turned his life around, Judge. He died in a car wreck trying to give Stephon a better life," Principal Davenport interjected, rolling her eyes hard at Rebecca.

"Mr. Johnson was one of the few young men who came out better than when he went in," the Judge noted. He caressed his beard, deep in reflection. "I think we're done here. I'll see everyone here this afternoon for Stephon's arraignment."

Rebecca scooted out of her chair aggressively, snatched her briefcase, and stormed out of the room. Principal Davenport and David exchanged looks of disdain.

"Let's get out of here before I become your next client," Principal Davenport muttered to David.

Later in the afternoon, the criminal courtrooms at 201 Poplar reopened after lunch break. A line snaked around outside the building leading to the entrance. The hallways reeked of disinfectant used to scrub yesterday's filth from the handrails, floors, and bathrooms. District Attorneys scurried from courtroom to courtroom with four-wheeled briefcases trailing behind them. Defense attorneys posted up in various corners discussing their cases with their clients. The entire scene resembled a busy third-world airport.

Inside Judge Wilson's courtroom, the families and friends of juveniles sat quietly awaiting arraignment. A few babies cried. Mostly African Americans and Hispanics were present. Plain-clothed and uniformed officers stood around the courtroom.

"All rise!" the bailiff bellowed. "The Court of Shelby County is now in session, the Honorable Judge Wilson presiding. Please be seated."

Judge Wilson limped into the courtroom using a cane, carrying a cup of coffee. The courtroom murmur quieted down. Judge Wilson opened a slender manila folder and thumbed through the paperwork.

"Your Honor, today's first case is The State of Tennessee v. Stephon Johnson, Case No. 15679. One count of unlawful possession of a firearm on school property," the courtroom clerk droned.

David and Rebecca moved from the gallery and approached the bench.

"David Miller for the Defendant, Your Honor."

"Rebecca Tanner for the government, Your Honor."

A uniformed police officer brought Stephon into the courtroom. He was handcuffed and dressed in an orange jumpsuit. He looked out into the crowd and found his sisters seated in the front row. The two became visibly upset when they noticed his black eye.

Principal Davenport sat in the row behind his sisters. Principal Davenport whispered words of encouragement to them.

"I will give counsel time to read the sworn affidavit that attempts to establish probable cause in this case," said Judge Wilson.

Both Rebecca and David quickly scanned the affidavit.

"Does the defense have any arguments against probable cause?" Judge Wilson interrupted.

"Yes, Your Honor," David said. "The affidavit states that a gun was found in my client's locker, but there is nothing else tying him to this gun. No admission of guilt. No fingerprint evidence. No eyewitness. Nothing. We all know that lockers are not foolproof. Anyone could have broken into my client's locker and put this gun there. In fact, the school uses the same combinations every year for its lockers. Who knows how many people had access to it?"

"Anything else, counsel?" Judge Wilson asked.

"No, Your Honor," David responded.

Stephon looked back at his sisters, who both dropped their heads in prayer. Stephon squeezed his eyes shut to avoid crying.

Judge Wilson rubbed his chin before he spoke. "I do find probable cause in this case. But I'm going to release Mr. Johnson into the community on condition that he attend school regularly and avoid any criminal activity." Judge Wilson looked directly at Stephon. "You're free to go." Stephon released a sigh of relief. He dropped his head and closed his eyes.

CHAPTER 18

Home Sweet Home

Laila's 2006 Honda Civic was parked outside Tall Trees Detention Center. Heavy rains poured down on her windshield. Flashes of lightning followed by crashes of thunder triggered car alarms in the parking lot. Tammy sat in the passenger seat, halfway reclined. Her neck-length braids rested on her shoulders like tiny black ropes leading to her brown scalp. Her tattoo-covered hands scrolled through Instagram. Laila sat in the driver's seat sporting a short Jada Pinkett-like fade with white AirPods plugged in her ears, listening to a podcast on criminal justice reform.

"Can you believe this kid Kalief Browder spent three years in prison for a crime he didn't commit?" Laila asked out loud.

"Mmhmm," Tammy mumbled, glued to her iPhone screen.

Laila continued, "They say the kid suffered from PTSD after what happened to him in that place. He killed himself."

"Oh yeah," Tammy nonchalantly responded.

"Tammy, are you even listening to me? Our brother just got out of jail and you're on Instagram watching Coachella replays. What is with you?"

"Don't start this shit with me, Laila. While you're running around Atlanta with professor-bae, Stephon and I are dealing with real problems. Shit you wouldn't understand."

"Problems you brought on yourself. Where do you think Stephon got the gun from? I told you about bringing niggas like TK around the house."

"Who the fuck are you to tell me who to be with?" yelled Tammy.

"Someone has to say something."

"If you are so perfect, why don't you bring your little girlfriend to the house so Granny can meet her?"

Laila turned her head away and looked out of the window, ignoring Tammy's rhetorical question.

"Right, I thought so. I know you like to think you're better than everybody in this family, but you're not!"

A hard knock on the back driver's side door startled them both. Stephon stood outside the car in the rain. Laila and Tammy exchanged bitter looks before Laila unlocked the doors. Stephon ripped open the back door and dropped into the seat, clothing drenched. Tammy reached for a hug. Laila turned around and smiled at him.

Stephon wiped water from his face. "All right, all right. I miss y'all too, but let's get out of here!"

Laila shifted the car into drive and slowly pulled off. She looked at Steph in the rearview mirror. "If you're hungry, we can stop somewhere on the way home."

"I'm good," Stephon murmured. "I just wanna go home."

Twenty-minutes later, Laila pulled into the broken concrete driveway beside their grandmother's shotgun home. The thirty-year-old shingle roof hung above the home in desperate need of repair. Black wrought-iron bars protected dirt-streaked windows.

The neighborhood was filled with rows of similar homes, mostly dilapidated. Neighbors sat outside on their front porches, enjoying the cool winds brought by the rains. Kids rode bikes up and down the street. Stephon stepped out of the car and inhaled a deep breath. Freedom had a smell now.

As he started toward the door, Rasheed slowly approached on a Mongoose bicycle spray-painted black so the real owner, and more importantly the police, couldn't identify it. Rasheed was the same age as Stephon, standing five feet nine inches tall with a body chiseled like a weightlifter. He lived two blocks over with his older brothers, PJ and Eric. All three brothers were members of the Memphis Lords.

Rasheed pulled up within a few feet of Stephon. He wore black Jordan retro 11s, black skinny jeans that fell slightly below his waist, and a white tank top that proudly exhibited his tattooed body.

Rasheed extended his fist. "Steph, what up?"

Stephon dapped Rasheed. "Same shit, different day."

"Heyyyyy Laila," Rasheed sang in a romantic tone, waving and smiling ear to ear. He suggestively licked his lips.

"Bye, Rasheed," Laila responded curtly as she stepped out of the car, purposely avoiding looking in his direction.

Tammy looked Rasheed up and down with scorn. "Shouldn't you be somewhere stealing bikes?"

Rasheed sucked his teeth. "Whatever, hello to you too."

Tammy looked at Stephon. "Don't keep Granny waiting."

Stephon nodded. "I got you." Tammy and Laila entered the house.

"First time at Tall Trees, huh? White Chocolate still acting hard over there?"

"Yep." Stephon sighed deeply.

"Man, don't even let that shit get to you. Everybody 'round here done some time at Tall Trees. You wasn't even supposed to be in there anyway."

Stephon flashed a puzzled look in Rasheed's direction. "What you mean?"

"Word is, that nigga Q, paid *somebody* to put that gun in your locker."

"What?!" Stephon fumed with anger, thinking about everything he went through because of Q. "How'd he get in my locker?"

"He found out who had your locker last year and got the code from them. Lazy-ass janitors never switched the combinations." Rasheed shook his head. "Anyway, you got bigger problems: folks saying you got beef with a nigga named Smoke."

Stephon paused for a minute, remembering the last words Smoke spoke to him before they both headed to solitary confinement.

"I ain't worried about them Frayser niggas."

"Shit, you need to be. If they catch you slipping, they gon' spin." Rasheed suddenly stopped talking and looked around for prying eyes. When he saw none, he pulled up his tank top and revealed the handle of a silver .40 caliber Ruger pressed to his torso. "I got 15 reasons niggas leave me alone."

They both turned when they heard the screen door to the house squeak open. Rasheed dropped his shirt quickly and waved to Stephon's grandmother, who stood in the doorway.

"Hey, g'am," Rasheed said. He put one foot onto his bike pedal and used the other to boost his momentum forward as he rode off into the street. He turned back towards Stephon. "Get up with me, Steph!"

Stephon smiled, concealing his concern and worry as he walked toward his grandmother's doorstep. She stood with arms folded under a heavy chest. She wore a floral-patterned gown and pink open-toe slippers. Her gray hair was covered with a blue headscarf.

"Stephon, get over here and give me a hug, boy," she commanded. Stephon walked over to his grandmother. She grabbed him with both arms wide open and squeezed the breath out of him. "Get inside. We need to get you some food." She curled her nose. "Seems like you could use some soap and water too, honey." She and Stephon both laughed.

Stephon pushed into his bedroom, sanctuary in a house that never felt quite like home. His prized sneakers—Nikes and Jordans earned through sweat and summer jobs—stood at attention beneath his twin bed like soldiers awaiting orders. The small flat screen and Xbox perched on his dresser, the only luxuries he could call his own.

His father's face smiled back at him from the makeshift nightstand—milk crates stacked with care, holding the one photo that mattered most. Camron, frozen in time, before everything changed.

Phone plugged in, shirt discarded, Stephon collapsed onto the mattress that had absorbed a thousand worries. His eyes had barely closed when the buzzing started—text after text lighting up his screen like fireworks. A weekend's worth of messages from a world that wouldn't let him rest.

He stared at the notifications flooding in and wondered if any of them actually mattered.

Friday 1:00 PM

Stats: Yo, you alright man? [concerned emoji]

Friday 8:00 PM

Stats: Don't drop the soap, my dude. [laughing emoji]

Stats: Bad joke, I know. Jk. Hit me up.

Friday 10:00 PM

Stats: Steph, seriously, hit me up when you get out of there.

Stats: We got a new head coach, bro.

Saturday 12:00 PM

Stats: Hit me up ASAP.

Saturday 1:30 PM

T.K.: Have you started reading the book I gave you? Don't let it go to waste.

Other notifications began to pop up as Stephon combed through his messages.

Commercial Appeal Breaking News: MLK hires former standout Lenny Chase as head coach.

Before he could read the article, he heard a loud scream from the living room. "What's going on?!" Stephon yelled as he rushed into the living room.

Laila, Tammy, and his grandmother were huddled on the couch. Tammy was crying. Laila looked up at Stephon. "TK's been shot."

"What?!" Stephon asked in disbelief. "Is he dead?" Laila responded with an affirmative head nod.

Stephon dropped his head and trudged back to his room. He sat on his bed, buried his face in his hands, and fought back tears.

CHAPTER 19

It's Your Move

Stephon opened his eyes slowly as the alarm on his phone chimed. He let GloRilla's "Yea Glo!" play a little longer. After a few minutes, Stephon dragged himself upright. A basketball waited in the corner like an old friend who refused to give up on him. He scooped it up and began the ritual—the same one he'd performed for three years, even when it no longer made sense.

Figure eights between his legs, head up, eyes tracking invisible defenders. Ten minutes flat on his back, perfecting the shooting form his father had drilled into his muscle memory until it became prayer. Then the defensive slides—doorway to window and back, fingertips brushing carpet like sidelines he'd never see again.

One hundred push-ups. One hundred sit-ups. Each rep a defiant whisper against the silence.

The game was over, but his body didn't know. Maybe it never would. In a world that had stripped away everything else, these movements were still his—untouchable, unbreakable, proof that some part of him remained unconquered.

After his workout, he quickly showered and got dressed. Before he could dart out of the house to catch the bus to school, he received a text message from Stats:

We gotta rap . . . meet me at the lockers, my guy.

Then a text from Sadat.

Sadat: Move my knight on the board to f5. I like that castle move; you're learning fast.

Sadat agreed to keep Stephon on as a client throughout his court case. As part of his ongoing therapy, Stephon agreed to play Sadat in chess on his phone. Sadat also requested that he create a duplicate game on the chessboard sitting next to his bed. "There is nothing like seeing the real thing," he said.

Stephon: My sister's boyfriend got killed this weekend.

Sadat: I'm sorry to hear that. I'm here if you want to talk about it.

Stephon: Preciate it, but gotta head to school.

Stephon slipped his phone into his pants pocket, moved Sadat's knight to f5 and his own bishop to d3, grabbed his backpack, and rushed out the door. He had only a few minutes to run three blocks and catch the school bus to MLK. As he turned onto the sidewalk, he could see the bus pulling away.

As Stephon cursed under his breath, he noticed an older model black Cadillac sedan with dark tinted windows pull up behind him. He watched the car out of the corner of his eye and looked around for potential escape routes. Just as he was about to make a run for it, Rasheed called out from a half-cracked window in the back seat of the car. "Steph, hop in, my nigga."

Stephon—relieved—walked around to the driver-side rear door, opened it, and climbed in. Rasheed's oldest brother, Eric, was driving. Rasheed's second eldest brother, PJ, sat in the passenger seat wearing sunglasses and rolling a blunt in his lap.

"What's good?" PJ asked. He continued rolling, sealing the blunt with his lips.

"Chilling," Stephon responded. He eyed a silver .44 Magnum wedged between PJ's seat and the console.

Rasheed recorded menacing facial expressions on Snapchat, showing off a new tattoo of the words "Memphis Lords" etched on his left and right eyelids.

"I told you not to get that dumb ass tattoo," Eric complained from the driver's seat.

Rasheed rolled his eyes and continued his social media showcase. PJ started to light the blunt in his right hand.

"Don't light that shit yet," Eric barked. "You want this nigga going to school smelling like dope? I swear y'all don't think." Eric looked at Steph through the rearview mirror.

"Steph, how's your sister doing? I heard about TK."

"She aight." Stephon watched the passing cars out the window.

Eric shook his head solemnly. "TK was a thorough nigga, but he was rolling solo out here. It was only a matter of time."

"Same shit I been telling Mr. MLK over here," Rasheed interjected.

"Shut up, fool," Eric said dismissively. Rasheed rolled his eyes but obeyed. "Steph, we got you, my nigga. Your pops was an OG back in the day. Whatever you need."

"Appreciate that, E."

Eric turned up the stereo's volume. Memphis rapper Coo Cash blared through the speakers as the four of them nodded their heads to the beat.

Eric pulled into MLK's parking lot behind a line of cars and buses. The school police presence prompted him to turn down the rattling bass.

"Aye, you can let me out right here, E. I appreciate the ride."

"No doubt."

"Sheed, you coming?" Stephon asked as he pulled himself from the car.

"Nah, I'm good. Got better shit to do than sit at a desk all day. Gotta get to the bag, fam."

Stephon nodded. "Aite."

As he walked toward the front of the school, Stephon saw Stats struggling to wheel his chair up the ramp next to the entrance. Students passing by knew Stats held too much pride to accept help. Almost in retrograde, Stats felt a sudden boost of power thrust him forward.

"What's up, Stats?" Stephon yelled as he pushed.

"Steph! What's good, my dude?" Stats looked back, smiling.

"Ain't much good, but I'm still here."

Stephon walked next to Stats as they moved through the hallway.

"Nigga, I feared the worst. Thought they had you on some Andy Dufresne shit."

Stephon's face was masked in confusion. "Nigga, who?"

"Andy Du-fr . . . never mind. I'm interviewing for a job tomorrow."

"Job?"

"Student assistant statistician." Stats beamed with pride as the two navigated his chair through a sea of students slamming lockers, rushing to class, and horsing around in the hallways. "The new coach been asking about you."

"Right now, I can't even think about basketball. I got too much shit going on."

The two stopped at Stephon's locker.

"Listen, I saw you put that gun in your locker, bruh." Stats whispered. "That was dumb."

"It wasn't a gun," Stephon responded in frustration. He reached into his locker, pulled out a book, and tossed it on Stats' lap.

"The Unapologetic Guide to Black Mental Health," Stats read the cover aloud in disbelief.

"TK gave it to me before he died. That's what you saw me put in the locker. That nigga Q set me up."

Suddenly, Stephon saw Principal Davenport charging in his direction. She held a bullhorn in her right hand and a walkie-talkie in her left. The last thing he wanted was another lecture about the choices that landed him in Tall Trees or someone else asking about his sister and TK.

"I gotta dip," Stephon told Stats, his eyes searching frantically for an escape.

Stats shook his head, confused. "We got history class now. Where you going?"

Stephon did a quick turnaround and made a sharp left down the north side of the school, where no classrooms existed. He stopped at the end of the hall near the double doors that opened to a staircase leading to the second floor. Students rarely used the stairs close to the end of the north hallway because they were poorly lit and lacked cameras. Most fights, drug activity, or worse occurred in this little corner—activity that earned it the moniker "the Trap."

Stephon started making his way up the Trap when he saw three students shooting dice on the landing. Wrinkled dollars were scattered across the floor.

"Five I shoot, here it come," rapped one of the students with a red bandana tied snug around his wrist.

Stephon heard dice hitting a wall. The other two boys were staring intently at the dice as they came to a stop. Each of the three wore just enough red for Stephon to know he had stumbled upon the wrong gathering.

"Aye, somebody's here," whispered one of the young men in the semi-circle. The three grabbed money from the ground, left the dice behind, and started to escape up the stairs.

Stephon noticed Q when he turned to grab his portion of the money. Stephon turned around to make his own escape.

"Hold up, hold up," Q said. "That's that bitch ass nigga Smoke got beef with." Q smiled devilishly. "Let's fuck this nigga up." The three bounded down the steps and charged toward Stephon.

He wanted to stand his ground, but Sadat's words cut through the noise.

'Life is chess. And chess is life.' Echoed in his head.

'There are times when taking pieces costs you more in the long run.'

'Retreating is not weakness.'

Stephon ran back toward the double doors he entered. He could hear the boys' laughter behind him. Just as he reached for the doors, they swung open, and he crashed into someone. He fell backward to the floor. He looked up. It was Lenny.

"My bad, just trying to get to class." Stephon stood up and dusted himself off.

Lenny leaned toward Stephon, extending a helping hand. "You're going in the wrong direction then. No junior classes on the first floor."

Stephon raised his eyebrows. "How you know I'm a junior?"

"I make it my business to know everything about my players, Stephon."

"I don't play ball anymore, coach."

Lenny whipped out his phone and showed Stephon his Tall Trees highlights. "Could've fooled me. Listen, come by the gym after school. What do you have to lose?"

Stephon shrugged. "I'll try."

Lenny shook his head. "Do. Or do not. There is no try."

Stephon pushed past Lenny, through the double doors, and into the hallway. His phone buzzed in his pocket. He pulled it out, and on the screen, there was a text message from

Sadat: It's your move

CHAPTER 20

Ball Don't Lie

Dressed in neatly pressed khakis and a dri-fit polo shirt with MLK across the chest, Lenny stood in front of his bedroom mirror and brushed his hair. Nas' "The World Is Yours" played from a Bluetooth speaker. Lenny rapped along in unison.

There was a soft knock at the door, but Lenny didn't hear it. The door slowly opened, and Patricia entered. She and Lenny's eyes met in the mirror. He stopped brushing his hair and turned around.

"Feels like my first day of school," Lenny said. "How do I look?"

"Tuck your shirt in and you'll be handsome," Patricia replied with a smile. Lenny hurriedly tucked his shirt in. Patricia sat down on the corner of his bed. "I'm proud of you." She wiped a tear from her eye. "Your daddy'd be proud too."

Lenny smiled slightly. "You think so?"

Patricia stood up and laid her hand on Lenny's shoulder. "I know so. Finish up and come downstairs. You can't start your first day of school without a good breakfast."

Inside his car, Lenny sat in silence. He gripped the steering wheel, his body paralyzed with nervousness. He grabbed a pint of Remy Martin from the glove compartment, hesitating at first out of guilt but eventually took a strong pull. The liquor relaxed him, relaxed his grip. Lenny took a second pull—not as heavy—returned the bottle to the glove compartment and popped a mint in his mouth. He addressed himself in the rearview mirror.

"I am the master of my fate; I am the captain of my soul."

Lenny pushed open the door to his new office. He flipped the light switch to reveal an empty room except for an ancient steel desk, a swivel chair, and two folding chairs. The paint on the walls was peeling. The carpet was threadbare. Wires jutted from the wall where someone had yanked the television free.

"Home sweet home." Lenny dropped his gym bag on the desk.

Tim poked his head into the office. "Knock knock." Lenny turned around. "Plush enough for ya," Tim joked.

"Top notch," Lenny responded with sarcasm.

"Huggy will work his magic on it. Just needs a coat of MLK love."

Lenny nodded. "It needs something."

"Budget cuts across all athletic programs." Tim sat in one of the metal chairs. "No money for assistant coaches, only volunteers."

"More good news." Lenny took a seat behind the desk.

"Well, the great news is that a former teammate of yours who happens to be Athletic Director is willing to volunteer for the assistant coaching position." Tim smiled broadly.

Lenny chuckled. "You're hired." Tim raised his fist in exultation. "We're a staff of two now."

"Three. There's someone I want you to meet." Tim turned around towards the door. "Stats, come in." Stats wheeled in. Tim turned back to Lenny. "Coach, this is Stats."

Stats beamed. "Sup, Coach?"

Lenny leaned back in his chair. "Why do they call you Stats?"

Stats sheepishly replied, "I'm good with numbers."

"He's a genius with analytics," Tim blurted out. "A genius."

"Really?" Lenny asked.

Stats nodded. He retrieved a tablet from his backpack and set it on the desk. Lenny scrolled through the Excel sheets. It was filled with diagrams, player profiles, stat sheets, and box scores. Lenny was impressed. "You made this?"

"Yeah, took me a couple of hours."

Lenny continued to scroll. "I can't have a winning team without a team manager. You know that, right?" Stats broke into a big smile and nodded in acknowledgment. "Welcome to the team, Stats."

Tim patted Stats on the back. Lenny handed back the tablet, exhaling deeply as he rested his chin in his hands. He looked at both Tim and Stats. "Fellas, we have a lot of work to do. It's going to be a late night."

The MLK Gym was dark, with only the red exit lights visible. Lenny stood at center court, holding a basketball. The gym, known as the "Box," was renowned throughout Memphis as one of the hardest places to win a game under Coach Heard. Visiting teams feared playing in the Box.

There was no air conditioning or heat, and no windows either. The bleachers were suffocatingly close to the court. The maximum capacity by law was 500 people, but on game days, that number was usually closer to 800, making it feel like a thousand. The entire neighborhood came out to the Box, and MLK fans were notorious for being unruly, offensive, and violent.

Lenny became a legend in the Box. So many great games flooded his memory: the last-second game-tying three-pointer against Memphis East in his freshman year, the 15-point fourth-quarter comeback win over Northside to clinch the division, and dropping 40 points against Cordova when they were ranked number two in Tennessee. The Box was home, a place filled with love, heartbreak, joy, and pain.

A loud clunk startled Lenny. The gym's lights slowly came up as Huggy entered through the double doors, pulling an industrial trash can. Huggy, a portly Black man with a cropped gray afro, wore paint-stained Dickies coveralls and steel-toe work boots. His right hand was severely mangled, and he always wore a batting glove to hide it from gawkers. Many myths surrounded how his hand became mangled, but none were verifiable. Huggy had worked at MLK as a janitor since before Lenny was a student.

Huggy spoke with a stutter, had a mouth full of gold teeth, and never missed an MLK basketball game. He bobbed his head to music in his headphones and didn't notice Lenny at first. He began pushing a dust mop across the floor when he looked up and saw Lenny. He smiled and slid the headphones off one ear.

"C-c-c-coach Chase!" Huggy exclaimed. Lenny smiled in return and walked over to him. They exchanged fist pounds.

"Good to see you, Huggy."

"G-g-glad you back home, Coach. Been too long since I hung a trophy. You gon' change that."

"Hopefully. I'm new to coaching."

Huggy gently poked Lenny in the chest. "Hoops in ya blood." He took the ball from Lenny, held it up to his face, and said, "Ball don't lie."

Lenny walked to his car in the empty parking lot behind the gym. He was surprised to find a battered banker's box sitting on the hood of his car, with COACH HEARD written in permanent marker across the top.

Now back home, under the gentle glow of a bedside lamp, Lenny lay across his bed and studied the Excel sheets that Stats emailed him. A basketball nudged between his feet. The sheets were excruciatingly detailed, breaking down every game from the previous season, including shooting percentages, perimeter defense ratings, offensive efficiency, and defensive stops gained. It was so much information that it was almost dizzying. Stats really was an analytics genius.

The game came to Lenny naturally. It was a gift, a sixth sense. He watched game footage of opponents, but he never studied numbers. He wasn't a student of the game. Now, he would have to be.

He shut his laptop and tossed it onto his bed. He grabbed the basketball from between his feet, flipped it in the air, caught it, and repeated the motion with a shooting gesture.

"Ball don't lie."

CHAPTER 21

Protect What You Love

Swish. Lenny loved that sound—a perfect shot hitting nothing but net. For Lenny, no sweeter sound existed. He retrieved the ball and walked back to the free-throw line. Lenny sank another one. Swish. In high school, Lenny shot until he missed. He led the state in free-throw shooting percentage his senior season. He loved the calmness of shooting free throws; it was the only time the game slowed down for him. Just him and the ball. He blocked out everyone and everything else.

"I call brick," shouted Principal Davenport, startling Lenny, causing him to miss his first shot all day. She walked toward him from the shadows of the gym, dressed casually in fitted jeans, a lightweight roll-neck sweater, and brightly colored Nike Air Max 1s. Her hair was covered by a well-worn baseball cap with Howard University embroidered across the front. She stopped a few feet from Lenny.

"Working on a Sunday, huh, Trina?"

"The gym is still on the MLK campus, so I'm still Principal Davenport," she reminded him jokingly, but with a hint of sincerity.

"*Excuse me*, Principal Davenport."

"You make it, I buy a round of drinks. You miss it, you buy a round of drinks. Deal?"

Lenny nodded with a smirk. "Deal."

Lenny turned toward the basket. Like a million times before, he dribbled twice, dipped slightly, and shot. The ball rolled around the rim and dropped in. He looked over at Principal Davenport with a cheshire grin. "Bring your wallet; I only drink the best."

Principal Davenport smiled in return and began walking toward the exit doors. "Let's go."

The sun was setting on a warm night as Lenny and Principal Davenport walked toward their cars. The parking lot was empty except for their two vehicles. In a parking spot with a sign reading "Reserved for Principal" sat a newer model cherry-red Mercedes Benz C-Class coupe.

Lenny stopped walking, pointed at the car, and shook his head in approval. "Wow, you out here stunting on folks!"

Principal Davenport blushed. "Stop it. It's only a C-Class." She stood beside the driver's door. "Alimony has its perks."

"Alimony?"

Principal Davenport opened the car door. "Let's get that drink." She slid into the driver's seat.

Sunday night at Sunnybrook was "Bourbon and Blues" night. Bourbon drinks were half-priced, and local musicians, usually amateurs, played blues songs. The bar was rarely crowded on Sundays, mostly hosting the usual hardcore drinkers, a few curious tourists, and working-class musicians.

Ty stood behind the bar, his muscular arms folded. Barrel-chested and strong as an ox, Ty played fullback on the University of Tennessee team that won the 1998 national championship. He didn't get drafted by an NFL team but signed with the Tennessee

Titans as an undrafted rookie, playing a few seasons before injuries derailed his career.

On the makeshift stage, Albert "Blue" Hunter warmed up on a beautiful Gibson Les Paul guitar borrowed from another musician. Blue was homeless and was regularly found begging for change on Poplar Avenue. Once a musical savant, he became a slave to crack during the early 1990s crack epidemic. Drugs stole his youth, derailed his career, and ended his marriage.

Blue was dark-skinned, lanky, and round-shouldered. He wore his hair cropped close, had a gaunt face, and missing front teeth. He donned dark sunglasses and was drowning in an ill-fitting suit that had been fashionable decades prior.

Lenny led Principal Davenport into Sunnybrook. They approached the bar, and Ty nodded in recognition. "Remy on ice for me," Lenny ordered. He looked to Principal Davenport.

"Make it two."

Ty nodded and went to pour the drinks.

Lenny looked surprised. "I didn't know you liked Remy."

"A lot you don't know about me. One is that I pay my bets." Principal Davenport pulled cash from her purse, and when Ty set the drinks down, she slid a twenty across the bar and grabbed the drinks. Lenny followed her to a table in the back.

As they sat down, Blue began playing a cover of Muddy Waters' "Honey Bee." Despite the drugs and despair, Blue still had it. He was an axeman. A few locals perked up and turned their attention to the stage.

Lenny raised his glass. "Cheers. To MLK. To new beginnings."

Principal Davenport raised her glass. "To a winning season."

They clinked glasses and each took a sip. Principal Davenport looked around the bar. "I remember we celebrated your 21st birthday here. You were sooo drunk." They both laughed nostalgically.

"That seems like a lifetime ago."

"I was in college. You were preparing for the draft. Jamel had that song with Crunchy Black that he swore was going to be a hit."

"Jamel still thinks that song is going to be a hit." They both laughed. "It was so simple back then. I miss those days."

Principal Davenport nodded in agreement. "It was much simpler. No mortgage, no bills, no divorce." She took a long sip of her drink.

"So tell me about this divorce?"

"What's there to tell? He cheated on me; I left. I won't play second fiddle. You know that."

Lenny looked down, stared into his drink, and finished it. "He was a fool. I know the girl didn't have anything on you."

Principal Davenport stood up. "It wasn't a girl, and you're right; he didn't have anything on me. Round two?"

Lenny's eyebrows raised as his eyes widened. "Damn. Yeah, make that a double."

Blue started into Buddy Guy's "What Kind of Woman Is This." A drunk lady in the audience stood, clapped, and shrieked, "Yes, lawd!" Blue was grooving, his body swaying as he played.

Principal Davenport returned with the drinks and sat down.

Lenny nodded in appreciation. "Thanks."

"You're welcome."

"So, what brought you back to Memphis, to MLK?"

"Honestly, my ex-husband brought me back to Memphis. We met in Nashville. He was in med school at Vandy when I was there getting my Master's. After we graduated, we moved back so he could finish his residency at Methodist. Until I met him, I was planning on going back to DC."

"No lie, I was jealous when I found out you were engaged. Facts."

Principal Davenport pressed her lips together, cutting her eyes slightly in Lenny's direction. "Not jealous enough to do anything about it. Facts."

"I was overseas, playing ball, trying to get to the NBA. You know how much I love ball. If anybody knows, you know."

Principal Davenport sipped her drink and looked at Lenny. "I came back to MLK because you protect what you love. You loved, love, basketball. You also told me you loved me." She finished her drink in a hurried gulp and stood up. "I need to leave."

Lenny stood up. "Wait. Trina, I'm sorry. I—"

"Stop, Lenny. I'm not here for sorries. I was a kid then. I'm a grown woman now. I don't need your sorries. You love ball? And you loved Coach Heard, right?"

Lenny shook his head. "Yeah, of course."

"Then protect what you love. See you tomorrow, Coach." Principal Davenport grabbed her purse and made her way to the exit. Lenny watched her leave as Blue charged into John Lee Hooker's "Hard Times." Instinctively, Lenny finished his drink and made a beeline for the bar.

CHAPTER 22

GAME 1

The buzzer sounded, waking Lenny from his daze. He sat up and took one final look at the scoreboard:

Cordova: 76, Guest: 46

In all the years Lenny played basketball; he never lost a game by 30 points. Truthfully, MLK could've lost by more. Cordova was led by one of the best frontcourt duos in the state of Tennessee: Chandler Temple III, aka CT3, and DeAndre Boone, aka DAB. Both were seniors and headed to play Division 1 basketball.

CT3, standing six foot nine, was lean, sinewy, and strong. He gobbled up rebounds and finished around the basket with ease. He signed with the University of Tennessee over the summer.

DAB, standing six foot eight and weighing 240 pounds, was brawny, with chiseled, tattooed arms. What he lacked in athleticism, he more than made up for with grit and hustle. He was often compared to former Memphis Grizzlies forward Zach Randolph. He was one of the rare high school players who enjoyed defense as much as scoring points. He signed with Georgia State.

Lenny shook his head in disappointment, shame, and embarrassment. He begrudgingly stood up to greet the opposing coaches and players with handshakes.

On the drive home, Lenny couldn't help but think about how different the game might have gone if Stephon had been playing.

While MLK proved little match for CT3 and DAB, Lenny knew Stephon would have had his way against them. Without a player like Stephon, the team's offense simply lacked firepower. They were lucky to have scored 46 points.

Tavon led MLK with 19 points. His steady play and smooth mid-range jumper impressed Lenny at times, but his selfishness and poor on-court leadership did not. If he could maintain a C average and score decently on the ACT, Lenny believed Tavon had Division I potential. Together, Tavon and Stephon could be a good, if not great, tag team, he thought.

Lenny pulled his car into the ShopRite parking lot. Two crack fiends, a man and a woman, argued on the sidewalk. A group of teens held up their phones and filmed it. The man punched the woman in the face, sending her crashing to the concrete. The teens laughed in glee.

The crack of fist on cheek made Lenny's stomach flip — old rage bubbled up before he could stop it. Lenny hopped out of the car. "Hey, what the hell is wrong with you?" he screamed at the man. The man looked startled.

"Mind your business, or you're next," one of the teens threatened. He was 16 but built like a grown man. His cornrows hung to his shoulders. He balled his fists up. The other teens turned their phones on Lenny. "We good or what?"

"I ain't the one, trust me."

The teens all laughed.

"Fall back, niggas," Stanley ordered as he walked out of ShopRite. He unscrewed the cap off a 40-ounce beer. "Y'all better recognize Memphis royalty. This is the great Lenny Chase—one of the best ballers ever to come out of the M."

"Stanley?" Lenny asked, starting to recognize the face.

"Been some years. Never thought I'd see you around these parts again," Stanley responded as he popped open a beer can. "How's Patricia?"

"Same old. Still on my back."

Stanley took a gulp and smiled. "Word is you're coaching at MLK now."

"Yep, first game was tonight. Took an L to Cordova."

"Fuck them Cordova niggas," Stanley drank. "Any niggas round here give you problems, holla at me. Wouldn't have it no other way for MLK fam."

"Appreciate that."

"Say less." The two dapped again, and Lenny walked into ShopRite.

CHAPTER 23

Be A Friend

BEEP, BEEP, BEEP. The oven buzzer sounded.

"Something smells good," Lenny exclaimed as he entered the kitchen. He filled an empty cup with homemade sweet tea from a glass pitcher.

Patricia sat at the kitchen table with her feet propped up, scrolling through Instagram photos of various gourmet dishes. Freddie Jackson's "Tasty Love" wafted through the kitchen from an Amazon Echo.

"Baked risotto with roasted vegetables," Patricia announced. "Just need to make the caprese salad."

"No chicken?" Lenny asked. He leaned back against the counter.

"I'm trying to get Eddie to cut back on meat," Patricia replied. "His cholesterol is too high."

"You really care for him, huh?" Lenny said.

Patricia nodded. "I do. It's been a long time since I cared for any man romantically." Patricia blushed. "Is that a problem?"

Lenny shook his head. "Not at all. Eddie is solid."

"I'm glad you think so. I have a feeling he'll be around a while."

Patricia got up, took a tomato from the fridge, and began slicing it with a serrated knife. "Tough loss yesterday. Cordova is good."

"Or we're bad. All we have is Tavon. That's not enough to win games. A game."

"How about the player that got caught up in that mess? You said he was really good."

"Stephon?" Lenny asked. "He doesn't want to play basketball anymore. He won't come to practice. The kid is throwing his career away."

"Didn't you say he had some problems at home?"

"Yeah, so does half of Memphis."

Patricia finished slicing the tomato and moved to slicing the burrata. "Some have it harder than others."

Lenny nodded. "He's got so much talent, but he's raw." Lenny stood up and refilled his cup. "If he would just let me, I know I can get him to the next level."

Patricia gave a half-smile as she wiped her hands. "Maybe what he needs isn't a coach, but a friend," Patricia said. The doorbell chimed. "That's Eddie." She finished slicing the burrata.

Lenny exhaled, wanting to argue — but found nothing left to say.

Patricia wiped her hands on her apron. She pointed at Lenny and repeated softly. "Don't be a coach. Be a friend."

CHAPTER 24

GAME 2

Lenny couldn't stop smiling as he shook hands with the Middle College players and coaches. He did a double take at the scoreboard.

Middle College: 45, Guest: 63

"Numero Uno," Tim said as he squeezed the back of Lenny's neck. "Numero Uno!"

Lenny nodded. "Monkey's off my back."

Middle College was an honors high school—a small school where academic success was prioritized over athletic success. The team won three games the previous season, so the victory was not impressive, but it was Lenny's first as a head coach.

Middle College was led by Richie Perkins, a scrawny 5'7" point guard with a mop of blonde hair and a deceptively quick first step. He was an unorthodox shooter—he brought the ball up to his chest and pushed it toward the basket. Perkins scored 25 points, mostly on open three-pointers and free throws.

Middle College led by four points after the first quarter. Lenny laid into the team, using enough expletives to fill a rap song. His rant seemed to spark something in Tavon, who exploded for 14 points in the second quarter. With a sizable height advantage over Perkins, his primary defender, Tavon drove to the lane with power, either finishing with an easy layup or drawing a foul.

When the eventual double teams came, he dished it to DaRon Scott on the block. DaRon's vertical jump and overall athleticism impressed Lenny. Despite his inconsistent mid-range jump shot, he had a soft touch around the rim.

DaRon ran the court with ease, and late in the third quarter, he sprinted down the baseline and connected with Tavon on an alley-oop that wowed the crowd. Tavon's pass appeared out of reach, but DaRon caught it with his outstretched hand and hammered down a dunk that made both teams stand up in awe. It was a SportsCenter highlight and the first time Lenny saw DaRon smile. And for good reason.

DaRon lived in a housing project in Frayser. He shared a mobile home with his mother, his toddler sister, and whatever new man was dating his mother. His mother worked two shifts as a nurse at local hospitals, and barely made enough to keep the lights on.

DaRon's father was killed by the police when he was younger. His three-year-old sister's father was Stix, a low-level drug dealer who sold expired prescription pills to college students. A year ago, Stix was arrested for selling Adderall to an undercover cop posing as a Rhodes College student. He jumped bail and drove off with DaRon's mother's 1995 Buick Park Avenue. Nobody has seen or heard from him since.

DaRon was reserved, spoke in mumbles, and never smiled. Lenny knew that DaRon's home life was a struggle, that money was tight, and that there was never enough—food, clothes, love. After he told Patricia about DaRon's living situation, she insisted he take him leftovers.

In the second half, Tavon continued his dominance. MLK began the third quarter on a 10-0 run, all scored by Tavon. Two long-range jumpers. A steal and fast-break layup. Two free throws.

A wide-open dunk off an outlet pass by small forward Terrence Price, one of MLK's most popular students, capped the run. With his perfect waves and dimples, he was fawned over by the girls at MLK. On the hardwood, Terrence played with effort and tenacity. He wasn't much of a scorer but always looked for the open man and hit the boards.

Terrence had a high basketball IQ, which Lenny appreciated. And he never lost his composure. He was a quiet leader, and Lenny relied on him to steer the team when they lost focus.

Terrence played basketball because he liked the sport. He planned to attend North Carolina A&T University for college and study engineering. He was a good student, always on the honor roll.

Lenny pulled Tavon midway through the fourth quarter. Tavon had scored 34 points, and after being called for his fourth foul, he began jawing at the referee. Tavon was the team's only reliable scorer, and rather than risk an ejection and possible suspension, Lenny sent him to the bench. Tavon rolled his eyes when Lenny called his name as he retreated to an open spot on the bench, scooted back loudly, and mumbled curse words underneath this breath. The rest of the fourth quarter was played by reserves, allowing some of the bench players some much-wanted minutes.

Lenny watched them ride the high, waving bags of chips like trophies. An NLE Choppa line thumped through the rattling windows: *"Walk em down, walk em down."* Lenny and Tim sat in the first two rows of the bus. Tim was on the phone, recapping the entire game to his wife. Lenny looked back at his players. There's no feeling like winning. Coach Heard said that before every game. Lenny watched his players riding the winning wave. He beamed with pride.

Lenny took another sip of Gatorade, tried to match their grins. It tasted flat.

Winning felt good — but without Stephon, it felt incomplete.

The next game was a home game. If Lenny could get Stephon to attend, then maybe he would see what he's missing. Maybe he would see the team's potential. Maybe he would see what MLK could be with him on the court.

CHAPTER 25

Hamlet

Stephon sat on his bed and flipped through an old SLAM magazine. He nodded his head to Kevo Muney's "Leave Some Day" playing from his phone. He put the magazine down, yanked his book bag up from the floor, and pulled out a stack of sealed envelopes. He sifted through the letters, each bearing the official logo of universities that were recruiting him before his father passed. All Division I schools, mostly in the South: Arkansas, LSU, Kentucky, Ole Miss, Memphis. After a standout summer sophomore season, ESPN ranked him top 20 in the country in his class. All the schools were after him.

That summer felt like a lifetime ago. Legendary Coach Eric Randolph had pulled every string to get Stephon transferred from East High to Florida Prep—a golden ticket to NBA dreams that his father had sacrificed everything to secure. The scholarship was still there, waiting like an open door to the future they'd mapped out together on countless car rides south.

But basketball died with his father on that highway.

Coach Randolph called every week, a gentle but persistent voice, reminding Stephon that the offer stood, that Camron would have wanted this. The words bounced off him like shots off the rim. Stephon had already made his choice the moment the funeral flowers wilted—he was done.

Back in his grandmother's house, surrounded by the smell of her cooking and the weight of unspoken grief, he buried his dreams alongside his father and swore the game would never hurt him again.

His phone vibrated. It was a notification from a chess app inviting him to continue a match with Sadat.

[MLKfinest has entered the chat room and game]

Sadat: You know, you're really picking up chess fast. I've never seen anyone come this close to beating me in just two weeks.

MLKfinest: My dad used to play. [white bishop from B1 to E4]

Sadat: Was he any good?

MLKfinest: He had a few trophies at our old house, so I guess.

Sadat: Who taught him to play? [Black pawn from C1 to F5]

MLKfinest: Some guy named Muhammed.

Sadat: Did you ever watch any of their games? Learn from him?

MLKfinest: Muhammed was my dad's cellmate. And nah, he only taught me one game, ball.

Sadat: When's the last time you talked to someone about your dad?

MLKfinest: Never. He was here, now he's gone. That's life. [white pawn from E2 to E3]

Sadat: And your mom?

MLKfinest: Met her a few times when she stops by asking granny for money. Sadat, what's up with the questions bro.

Sadat: [checkmate! Black Rook from F8 to C2] Gametime.

MLKfinest: Damn, smh.

Sadat: Once your opponent gets in your head, it's only a matter of time before your king falls. Want to know what separates good chess players from great ones?

MLKfinest: Focus? Block out distractions . . .

Sadat: Yes, but not by pretending they don't exist. By embracing the reality that the only thing you can control about adversity is how you respond to it.

[Game ended by MLKfinest. Your chat room has closed.]

Stephon closed the app and set his phone on the charger with deliberate care, like everything else might shatter if he moved too fast. He collapsed back onto his bed, eyes fixed on the water stain spreading across the ceiling like a map of nowhere.

The photograph pulled his gaze like gravity—the only one he'd salvaged from the wreckage. Fab 48 in Vegas, five years ago when the world still made sense. Eleven-year-old Stephon grinning beside his father, Camron's hand resting on his shoulder like a blessing. The other hand holding that first MVP trophy, the one that started it all.

He'd dominated kids two years older that summer—fifteen points, seven assists, two steals per game. Numbers that once meant everything, now just ghosts haunting a dead dream.

Stephon reached for the frame with trembling fingers, Camron's proud smile burning through him like acid. The tears came in waves—first just moisture at the corners of his eyes, then unstoppable floods that shook his shoulders and stole his breath.

In that photograph, his father was still alive, still believing, still convinced his son would conquer the world.

Then he heard a faint knock on the door and hurriedly wiped his eyes.

"Yeah?"

The door inched open, and Laila called in, "You sleep?"

"Nah, I'm up."

Laila walked in and sat on the edge of his bed. Stephon stopped the music playing from his phone.

"I'm driving back to school early in the morning. Just wanted to say goodbye before I leave."

Stephon looked back at the photo of him and his father. "You ever think about how different life would be if he were still here?"

Laila got up, walked over to Stephon's dresser, and picked up the photo. "Sometimes, yeah." Laila laughed. "Before you were born, he used to try to teach Tammy and me to play basketball. Tammy quit after one practice. I tried to stick with it, but he could tell my heart wasn't in it, so he just stopped taking me to games. Then you came . . ."

" . . . yeah, then I came and ruined his life. Shit, everybody's."

Laila was taken aback by Stephon's comment. "What? Where is this coming from?"

"He died helping with my dreams, Laila. Trying to make sure I got to Florida."

"And you think that's your fault?"

"He ain't here, is he?"

"Do you remember when you were in the 7th grade and you got in trouble at school?"

"Yeah, I remember."

"Dad made you try out for that Shakespeare play as punishment because he knew you hated public speaking and being on stage."

Stephon nodded in agreement with a half smirk.

"We stayed up all night helping you with your lines. Dad kept repeating them in a fake 16th-century English accent."

Stephon and Laila shared a laugh. "Yeah, I hated that ugly-ass costume I had to wear."

"There is nothing either good or bad, but thinking makes it so," they both recited in unison with exaggerated English accents.

Laila hugged Stephon tightly. "It's up to us to make the best of our lives with Mom and Dad gone. This life is what it is. Blaming yourself only makes it worse."

Stephon nodded.

"Dad is up there watching over you, over us. He doesn't want you blaming yourself. He wants you playing basketball and honoring him, his legacy."

"Think so?"

"Of course." Laila stood and kissed Stephon on the forehead. "I'll be home for winter break. Love you, little bro."

"Love you too, sis."

CHAPTER 26

Superstars

It was a rainy Saturday morning following the team's win over Middle College. Lenny stood at the free throw line facing the team. Drenched in sweat, the players were bent over, gasping for air, fighting exhaustion.

"You guys win one game—one," Lenny snarled. "Now you're the damn Lakers. Down and back. Go!"

A group of seven shirtless players sprinted from the baseline past Lenny. The screeching of sneakers filled the gym. DaRon, Tavon, and Terrence all ran shoulder to shoulder leading the first group.

"Coach, make sure them boys touch that line down there, or we're starting over."

"I got you, coach," yelled Tim, standing on the opposite baseline, watching the line like a hawk. "All the way to the line, fellas!"

"Coach, how many we gonna run, damn," Tavon groaned.

"As many as it takes," Lenny responded before blowing his whistle for the next group to sprint. "You boys are gonna learn. There ain't no superstars on this team!"

The second group made its way back to the baseline. Tavon, Terrence, and DaRon started towards the edge of the baseline with fists balled, knees bent, and heads bowed, preparing for another sprint. Suddenly, Lenny noticed the players standing up straight.

Everyone was looking towards the gym's entrance. When Lenny turned around, he saw Stephon standing near the double doors.

Terrence tapped an exhausted, down-facing Tavon on the back and pointed in Stephon's direction with an incredulous frown. "You see this shit?" Tavon stood up straight and folded his arms as he watched Lenny walk towards the entrance.

"Free throws on both ends. Two, then rotate. After that, water break," Lenny ordered.

Lenny slowly made his way over to the entrance. The players watched out of the corner of their eyes while pretending to care about shooting free throws.

"Stephon Johnson, to what do we owe this honor?"

"Just stopping by the gym, that's all."

"On a rainy Saturday morning? You must really love this gym son."

Stephon sheepishly nodded. "I guess so."

Stephon looked over at the scorer's table and noticed Stats sitting in his wheelchair, crunching numbers on his computer. The two locked eyes before Stats quickly averted his gaze back to his task.

"Let's go to my office so we can talk."

Lenny's office had transformed from condemned wreck to something approaching respectable. He and Huggy had spent an entire weekend sweating through the renovation, their handyman skills tested to the breaking point. Gone was the moldy carpet that reeked of decades-old disappointment—sleek laminate flooring now caught the afternoon light streaming through clean windows. Fresh white paint erased years of neglect from the walls.

The cherrywood desk—a Goodwill treasure Huggy had spotted and haggled down to twenty bucks—commanded the center of the room like it belonged in a real office. A beige couch faced it, ready for the kids who would eventually find their way here, looking for guidance or just someone who understood.

But the walls told the real story. Medals and trophies from his playing days created a constellation of past glory, each one a reminder of what was possible. Above his reclining chair hung the crown jewel—him and Coach Heard hoisting the state championship trophy, both of them frozen in that perfect moment when everything still lay ahead.

The office looked professional now. Whether Lenny could live up to it remained to be seen.

"You remember Coach Heard?" Lenny reclined back in his chair, pointing at the photo behind him.

"Naw, but my dad used to talk about him when he took me to games. Said he was the best coach in the city."

"No doubt. You know why?"

Stephon shrugged his shoulders.

"He treated every single player like his own son." Lenny smiled. "Family first. School. Then, basketball."

Stephon pursed his lips.

"Listen, Stephon. Forget basketball. How are you doing? I know you've been through a lot lately."

Stephon looked down blankly at his Jordan Retro 6s and shrugged.

Lenny reclined back in his chair, placing his hands in prayer position right below his lower lip. "Look, I'm here for you. Not just as a coach, but as a friend. I know what it's like to lose a father and to feel like the whole world is against you. I also know what it's like to not be able to play the game you love."

Stephon looked up at Lenny, his posture softened. "I see you guys finally got a win."

Lenny cracked a smile. "First win of the season, but we got a long way to go. No way we're making the playoffs with our defense. And besides Tavon, no one can really create their own shot."

Stephon sat up, alert. "Tavon can score, but what people don't know is that he likes passing more."

"Could have fooled me," Lenny chuckled.

"Terrence can lock down anyone, I mean any—body. I've seen him put All-Americans in the trunk. But he's only motivated when he's mad." Stephon's speech sped up with excitement. "DaRon can outjump anyone in Memphis. His pick and roll game is better than anyone I've seen too."

Lenny nodded, impressed. "Where was all this when I was looking for an assistant? You want Tim's job?"

Stephon laughed. "I'll pass."

"I tell you what... I have a job you might actually want." Lenny leaned forward in his seat, opened his desk drawer, pulled out a practice jersey, and tossed it to Stephon, who caught it. "How about team captain?"

Stephon raised the jersey up.

"I figured I'd save number one for you. I watched your old man play back in the day; same number, right?"

Stephon nodded his head. His heart thumped with pride as he eyeballed the jersey. He could hear his father's voice in the room, bragging about his old games.

"One of the best to come out of Hilcrest." Lenny exclaimed. Then he stood up. "No pressure. Just think about it."

Back in the gym, Lenny watched Tim struggle to keep the team in order. Players were horsing around behind Tim's back during drills, while others stood on the sidelines cracking jokes.

Lenny shook his head and sighed. "I see we still haven't gotten the message. Everybody back on the line!" Groans filled the gym as the players slowly made their way to the baseline. "First group up!"

Terrence and DaRon filled in the middle of the first group of sprinters. Tavon begrudgingly filled in the last spot on the baseline. Right before the whistle blew, Stephon appeared next to Tavon, wearing a practice jersey. Tavon's focus intensified. He nudged Stephon with his shoulder to create space.

"Coach, I thought you said there weren't no superstars on this team," Tavon asked with a sarcastic tone.

Lenny smiled. "Shut up and run, Tavon. Go!"

Stephon took off in front of the pack with long athletic strides, beating everyone else back to the baseline with plenty of time to spare. Tim and Lenny looked at each other. Tim winked, and Lenny smiled while mumbling under his breath, "We do now."

CHAPTER 27

Steps Ahead

S adat sat alone on a bench in Overton Park in East Memphis. A
chessboard was painted on the concrete table in front of him.
He removed a roll of paper towels from his backpack and wiped
down the table. Then, he opened a clear ziplock bag of chess pieces
and dumped them onto the table.

As he arranged the chess pieces, he watched Stephon climb out
of Tammy's car and head toward him. Sadat gestured for Stephon
to sit. Stephon sat and quietly looked over the chess pieces.

"I'll be honest, I'm surprised you showed up," Sadat said with a
smile.

"Needed to get out of that house," Stephon replied as he
touched one of the pieces. "I joined the team yesterday."

"Back hoopin, huh?" Sadat smiled. "It was only a matter of
time."

"Why you say that?"

"There's our plan. And then. There's Allah's plan, son."

Words Stephon's father uttered to him more than once. Silence
filled the air for a few seconds until Sadat's words broke it.

"Nothing like the real thing." Sadat pointed to the board.
"Seeing your opponent across from you. The handshake after
defeat,"

Stephon shrugged indifferently.

Sadat set up his side of the board. He raised the knight in the air. "My favorite piece."

Stephon looked up. "Why?"

Sadat folded his hands in his lap. "Because he's unorthodox; opponents never see it coming."

Stephon looked down at the board and picked up the bishop. "My dad's favorite."

"Not a bad choice. His reach is long, and he can protect your king from afar." Sadat noticed Stephon take a deep breath. More than chess was on his mind. A moment of silence passed between them.

"If you can master chess, you can master life," Sadat said, breaking the silence. "Go ahead; you're white."

Stephon hesitated and then moved a pawn positioned in the middle of the board forward two spaces.

"Why did you move that piece?" Sadat asked.

"I don't know. It's just the first move," Stephon answered defensively.

"Never make a move without a plan, because every move you make will determine whether you win or lose," Sadat said calmly.

Stephon shrugged. "What if you don't know what move to make?"

"Then you'd better study someone who does," Sadat replied before he moved his knight out from the rear, challenging Stephon's pawn.

Stephon had never experienced anything like this. Online chess was just pixels and algorithms but sitting across from Sadat—breathing the same air, reading the micro-expressions that flickered across his face—felt like discovering a new language.

He'd never shared silence with another man like this, not even his father, it was comfortable and charged at the same time. Hours dissolved into minutes as they hunched over sixty-four squares, each lost in the other's mind. Stephon's arms rested on the worn table, his eyes tracing the board like a battlefield map, calculating three moves ahead while trying to decipher the slight furrow in Sadat's brow.

This wasn't just a game—it was warfare fought with intellect instead of fists, respect earned through clever sacrifices and patient builds. They dissected openings until Stephon could see the poetry in a well-executed Sicilian Defense. Middle game tactics became conversations without words. Endgames taught him that sometimes winning meant knowing when to let go.

When Tammy's horn cut through the evening air, Stephon realized the sun had nearly set. Two hours had felt like two minutes—or maybe two lifetimes.

"Let's go, Steph," Tammy yelled out the car window.

Stephon groaned but stood up.

Sadat stood as well. "Remember, chess and life are a thinking man's game. Never respond with emotions. If your opponent sees that, he's got you. If I take your queen, act like you planned it that way."

Stephon nodded in understanding. "I'm out. Appreciate the lessons."

Sadat extended his hand. Stephon shook it. "The pleasure was all mine, son. Stay a few steps ahead of your opponent, and they'll never see you coming."

Stephon nodded and sprinted to Tammy's car just as she honked the horn again.

CHAPTER 28

GAME 3

Inside MLK's gym, a near-capacity crowd continued to grow as fans filed in. The smell of popcorn, melted cheese, and smoked sausages drifted from the concession stand into the arena. Police officers stood guard near the exits. Officer Booker stood near the entrance, watching as people entered through the metal detectors. His left hand cradled a box of popcorn that he lifted towards his tilted head, dumping kernels into his mouth.

"I ain't seen this many folks in this gym since Coach Heard was coaching," Officer Booker mumbled to Principal Davenport, who stood next to him against the wall. "I see why y'all wanted the Stephon kid back so bad."

"You worry about the popcorn you keep dropping on the court and making sure no one brings a gun into this game. I'll focus on the rest."

Officer Booker nodded in affirmation. "You got it, boss."

INSIDE MLK's boys' locker room, Tavon dribbled a basketball between his legs, up and down the floor with AirPods in his ears. DaRon sat in front of his locker, legs spread out, stretching his lanky arms in opposite directions towards each toe.

Harrison Fields, a spindly 6'2 sophomore guard who dressed for both JV and varsity games, stood in front of his locker. Stephon stood at the locker next to his, slowly rocking back and forth. "Nervous?" Harrison asked. Stephon shook his head no but continued rocking.

Tim stood at the door and heard a faint knock. He pushed open the door, and Stats wheeled into the locker room with his laptop in tow.

"Guys, Frayser is trash from the line," Stats began. "65%, but they drain threes, especially number 10, Frank Thomas. He's 45% from the corner." Barely anyone acknowledged Stats as he rattled off numbers from his scouting report.

"Aye, man, y'all need to listen up," Stephon shouted. "Stats knows his stuff. This ain't Middle College; these folks can play."

Stats glanced up from his laptop in Stephon's direction with a look of appreciation.

Tavon removed one of his AirPods. "So, you the coach now?"

"Naw. I'm just saying we got ten minutes before tipoff and y'all look scared."

Tavon dropped the ball and approached Stephon's locker. Harrison slid out of the way. "Scared? Bruh, where were you the first two games of the season?"

Stephon stood up from his locker, hovering a few inches over Tavon. The rest of the team watched with anticipation. Tim walked over and stood between the two. "Chill out, you're teammates," he said.

Lenny burst into the locker room. "Everybody on their feet!" He noticed the standoff between Stephon and Tavon. "Tavon! Stephon! Good to see y'all bonding. Now get your asses over here so we can go over this game plan."

Stephon and Tavon stared at each other for a few more seconds before walking over to the whiteboard, where Lenny began drawing up plays.

TIP OFF. A single referee tossed the ball high into the air between DaRon and Frayser's tallest player, 6'6" center River Parks, a player notorious for his dirty play.

Stephon watched Lenny from the bench. He noticed the small imprint of a flask in Lenny's left pocket as he paced up and down the sideline. Stephon observed Lenny sweating profusely while struggling to keep his balance. Lenny seemed different from practice, but no one else seemed to care, so Stephon focused his attention back on the game.

Out there on the court, the accuracy of Stats' scouting report appeared undeniable. Frayser jumped out to an early lead behind a barrage of Frank Thomas three-pointers. Thomas, a 6'3" athletic guard with a Boosie-fade, moved quickly without the ball, finding just enough space to launch his unorthodox set-shot towards the rim. He barely left the ground on his shot, but it didn't matter because his height and quick release made his shot unblock-able. The score was 9-2 Frayser as Frank sank a step-back three in Terrence's face, then turned to taunt MLK's bench with the follow-through.

Tavon rushed the ball up the court, weaving through Frayser's three-quarter court trap. A lane to the basket appeared to open until a Frayser guard poked Tavon's dribble from behind, causing him to lose the ball. Parks scooped it up and shoveled it to Frayser's point guard, Ray Ray. Ray Ray shook DaRon with a quick in-and-out crossover and blew past him in the opposite direction. Terrence galloped toward MLK's basket for a chase-down block, but Ray Ray pump-faked him in the air and passed it off to Frank for an open layup. 11-2 Frayser.

"Shit! Come on, Tavon, pass the ball, son!" yelled Lenny.

From the bench, Stephon shook his head in disappointment. As his eyes shifted toward the crowd, a wave of fear passed through his body. He could see Smoke entering through the metal detectors. A group of Frayser Fiends followed behind him, including Q and two other boys Stephon recognized from the dice game. Q spoke into Smoke's ear while pointing in Stephon's direction.

Frayser's coach signaled for a timeout. Terrence, Tavon, DaRon, Harrison, and Tony—a 6'3" junior guard—sprinted to the sideline to greet Lenny.

"You guys are playing like pure shit right now," Lenny growled. "Tavon, I guess you didn't learn anything from all that running on Saturday, huh? Pass the damn ball, son!"

Stephon continued staring away from the huddle, glancing in Smoke and Q's direction.

"Stephon! Pay attention, dammit. I said go check in." Lenny fumed.

"Yes, coach." Stephon threw off his warm-up top and sprinted toward the scorer's table.

Stephon stepped onto the court and tucked his jersey into his shorts. He wiped the soles of his Gatorade green Jordan Retro 6s before entering the game. He took an entry pass from Harrison on the wing with River Parks guarding. Stephon pump-faked, causing Parks to leave his feet as Stephon breezed past him. One powerful dribble, and he took off from the baseline on one foot, dunking the ball with ease. When he turned around, he locked eyes with Parks and winked. 11-5 Frayser.

Stephon's offensive play revived MLK's defensive energy. DaRon slapped the floor and squatted low to the ground while face-guarding Parks closely. Lenny flashed an "X" symbol with his forearms while yelling "X" from the sideline, a signal for a half-court trap. Immediately, Tony and Terrence rushed one of Frayser's guards, trapping him as he stepped across half court. Tony and Terrence's long arms blocked the player's view as he began to fall back on his heels near the centerline.

The guard launched a two-handed pass toward Frank, but DaRon stepped in and intercepted the ball. DaRon took a few long strides past half court and finished with a finger roll high above the rim. 11-7 Frayser. The first quarter ended.

FOURTH QUARTER

Three quarters of tight basketball flew by, and the teams entered the fourth quarter tied at 55-55. Cheers and boos from the crowd intensified with each play as the final period reached the four-minute mark. Frayser's coach called a timeout when he saw his team struggling to inbound against MLK's full-court press. Tavon, Stephon, DaRon, Terrence, and Tony rushed to the sideline, out of breath.

"Listen, we're only down three points. Let's run . . . let's run Flex . . ." The team stared at Lenny's clipboard, confused, marker trembling uncontrollably. Sweat dripped from Lenny's head. His entire suit was drenched in perspiration, which smelled of alcohol.

He scribbled an illegible play on the whiteboard, struggling to remember the details.

"Coach, we're on defense right now," Stephon corrected him.

"Right, run 2-3, and after the rebound, run flex on the right side to DaRon."

"You sure, coach?" Tavon asked. "They're shooting lights out."

Lenny shot Tavon an angry look. "Yes, I'm sure!"

The horn sounded. Tavon and Tony positioned themselves in the backcourt, just above both elbows. DaRon stood with his head underneath the basket. Stephon and Terrence stood opposite each other on the baseline, guarding the corners of the zone. The clock started. All of them sat in defensive stances with arms extended.

When Frayser's coach saw how MLK was set up, he called out a new play from the sideline. Ray Ray dribbled quickly to the top of the key, pulling both Tavon and Tony toward him. Meanwhile, Parks slipped out to the wing for a pass, and Frank Thomas drifted down by the baseline, waiting for an opening.

Stephon stuck close to Frank, not wanting to give up an easy three. That left a gap in the middle, and Parks saw it. He drove straight down the lane, pulled up, and knocked down a wide-open jumper before DaRon could get there. Swish. 66-61, Frayser.

Frayser immediately set up their full-court press defense. Tavon broke free and caught an entry pass from DaRon. Frayser trapped him in the corner, but Tavon launched a baseball pass to Stephon, standing at center court. Stephon jumped high in the air to avoid a turnover and snagged the ball. He turned and dribbled past his defender before raising up at the top of the key for a three-pointer. Bank shot. 66-64 Frayser. Fifty seconds left on the clock.

"2-3 zone," barked Lenny.

Stephon ignored him and locked eyes with Tavon. "Let's go, man."

Tavon shook his head in agreement. "Man up!" he yelled as he backpedaled on defense. "Man, man, man."

Lenny turned to Tim, puzzled. Tim shrugged his shoulders. Lenny folded his arms and remained quiet.

Frayser spread the court. Ray Ray dribbled the ball low to the ground near half court, eyeing the clock as it ticked down to twenty seconds. Frayser's plan was simple: hold the ball.

Tavon lunged at Ray Ray's dribble, forcing him to spin away and shield the ball. Tony saw his chance—abandoning Frank on the wing, he sprinted to trap Ray Ray at half court. The walls closed in.

Ray Ray spun back; eyes wide as the double team descended. He lobbed an overhead pass toward Frank, but Stephon read it perfectly, snatching the ball mid-flight and exploding up the sideline like a man possessed.

Eight seconds. Ray Ray was the last line of defense, charging at Stephon with desperate arms reaching for anything—jersey, skin, basketball. Before contact came, Stephon launched himself skyward and fired a pass to Tavon, who stood alone beyond the arc like he was waiting for destiny.

Two seconds. The gym held its breath.

Tavon's shot climbed toward the rafters, spinning end over end—a prayer wrapped in leather and hope. Every soul in the building rose as one, time suspended in that impossible moment between heartbreak and glory.

Swish.

The building exploded. MLK 67, Frayser 66. Drake's voice thundered through the speakers as fans poured onto the court like water through a broken dam, drowning the defeated in celebration.

CHAPTER 29

Teammates

After several minutes of chaos, the crowd at MLK began to disperse. The lights were dim, except for a few floodlights. Most of the players from both teams had made their way to their locker rooms, with only Stephon left pushing Stats toward the back. As they made their way to the door, Stephon heard a familiar voice behind him.

"I lost bread tonight," the voice insisted.

Stephon turned around and saw Smoke standing in an all-black hoodie with matching jeans and red Jordan 11s, beside Q and two other gang members.

"Your fault; nobody told you to bet against us," Stats retorted.

Stephon nudged Stats to be quiet and whispered for him to go back in the locker room.

As Stats wheeled himself past Q toward the locker room, Q grinned. "Was I talking to you, waterboy?"

Smoke peeled away from the pack, fists already clenched, Q and two others forming a wall of malice behind him. They'd positioned themselves perfectly—Stephon's back to the hallway, their bodies blocking his only path to the locker room. Trapped.

No running this time. No teachers. No witnesses.

Stephon's mind shifted into chess mode, calculating angles and possibilities like Sadat had drilled into him. Three moves ahead, always three moves ahead. His left foot slid forward, right foot back—the stance his father had made him practice until muscle memory took over. The familiar weight distribution felt like armor.

One truth crystallized: he could drop Smoke with the right shot, but four against one was mathematics, not fighting. He needed to hit hard enough to plant doubt in the others, create just enough chaos to slip through the cracks. Make them hesitate. Make them remember that cornered animals bite deepest.

Smoke's sneer widened as he closed the distance. Time to find out if all those lessons—from his father, from Sadat, from the streets themselves—had taught him how to survive this moment.

Just as Smoke began to walk toward Stephon, the locker room door swung open, and Tavon, DaRon, Terrence, and Tony rushed out, jumping in front of Stephon. Tavon was the first in line and stood face to face with Smoke, unflinching. DaRon, Terrence, and Tony towered over Q and the other boys, their muscles on display.

"How y'all wanna do this?" Tavon asked. "Y'all Frayser niggas don't scare us."

Both sides could feel the tension rise. One wrong move would set off a melee. Tavon was itching to throw the first punch. Within seconds, Lenny and Tim burst through the locker room door into the gym, with Stats wheeling behind them.

"Hey! What the hell is going on out here!" Lenny shouted as he ran toward the group. Before he got there, Q grabbed Smoke by the shirt and nodded toward the exit as his crew scrambled away. Tim chased after them. Lenny watched as they disappeared. After a few seconds, he turned toward his players.

"Somebody wanna tell me what the hell happened?" Lenny barked.

Tavon, DaRon, Terrence, and Tony kept quiet and avoided eye contact. Stephon spoke up. "We are good, coach. My teammates had my back." Stats smiled as the group walked back to the locker room together. Lenny stayed behind, standing in the middle of the court with his arms folded.

Tim returned out of breath. "What'd you find out?" he asked Lenny.

"That I'm going to need some reinforcements," Lenny pondered.

CHAPTER 30

Da Game Owes Me

Earlier that morning, Lenny couldn't shake the image of Smoke staring down Stephon after the game. He knew the streets didn't play fair, and if Smoke was involved, this wasn't going away quietly. Lenny rapped along to Playa Fly's "Da Game Owes Me" as he pulled into the Shoprite parking lot. The same group of young men he ran into after the Cordova game were standing outside the store. Lenny turned off the car and hopped out.

As he approached the teens, they immediately steadied themselves with menacing stares. Lenny recognized their defensive reactions. He slowed his walk. "Y'all seen Stanley?" he asked.

A skinny teen with long braids dressed in a black hoodie and sagging stone-washed jeans stepped from the pack. He looked Lenny up and down.

"Hellcat?" he said, glancing at Lenny's car.

"I wish. Any of y'all know where Stanley's at?"

"Stanley over there on Trigg with the other big homies."

"Appreciate that. You got size on you. We could use another big man at MLK. You play ball?" Lenny asked.

The young man's menacing gaze softened. His eyebrows raised briefly as he stared at Lenny. "A little," he replied. Before the kid could get another word in, a chunky middle schooler tapped him on the shoulder. "Man, let's roll." And the two walked away.

Lenny pulled out of the parking lot and headed south on Mississippi Boulevard. He cruised past vacant storefronts, empty lots with uncut weeds, stop signs covered in graffiti, and dilapidated shotgun homes. South Memphis was one of the neighborhoods left behind—the birthplace of blues, soul, and gospel; home to one of the most famous record labels in history, Stax Records; now left to die after decades of neglect.

When Lenny pulled onto Trigg, he spotted a group of neighborhood drunks sitting on egg crates, drinking beers in brown paper bags. Lenny parked in front of Stanley's row house as the group flashed skeptical stares in his direction.

A middle-aged man with charcoal skin and a grizzly face approached Lenny. "You lost, young blood?"

"Looking for Stanley."

"You that new MLK coach, ain't you?" croaked a lanky man with teeth like broken picket fences. "Hell yeah, I remember. This cat was the truth — ran with Coach Heard's squad."

Stanley pushed his way through the group. "Lenny, what you doing down here?" Stanley turned to the drunks. "Y'all get off my yard and find somewhere else to waste your time." The crowd began to disperse.

With a nod, Stanley motioned for Lenny to follow him. They climbed up the crumbling steps to Stanley's porch and sat down on two flimsy plastic lawn chairs. Stanley opened a metal cooler that sat between the chairs. Miller Lite cans were swimming in water.

"Cool one?"

"Nah, appreciate it," Lenny rejected, wishing he could accept the offer. He could taste the liquor on the tip of his tongue. "Busy street, I see."

"Most of those guys had some hoop dream. Now, they're mad at the world, thinking the game still owes them something. But it don't."

Lenny nodded in approval but felt the stinging truth of Stanley's words.

"That's Memphis for ya. Only a few gonna make it out." Stanley took a sip of his beer. "What got you in the belly of the beast on a Saturday morning?"

"I got a kid who has a shot to be great. I'm talking really great."

Stanley finished his beer and placed the empty can on the porch floor.

"But I think he's caught up in some mess with these Frayser Fiends. Kid has too much going on to focus on basketball."

"What's his name?"

"Stephon Johnson."

"Stephon Johnson, huh? Name sounds familiar. Cam Johnson's kid?" Stanley asked.

"That's him."

Stanley sat back in his chair, contemplative. An awkward silence filled the air as he stared into the sky.

"You know, Patricia was right to cut me off when she did. Best woman I ever dated, to this day. She always put you first. You were too little to remember, but I'm the one who taught you that jump shot." Stanley laughed.

He took another beer from the cooler and stood up. "Say no more. It's taken care of."

"Really?"

Stanley nodded. "It's the least I can do."

"Appreciate that." Lenny stood up from his chair and embraced him with a handshake hug. "I'm going to get at you a little later. I got practice in an hour."

"Bet." Stanley lifted his beer bottle in salute as Lenny walked toward his car. "Oh, and Lenny," Stanley pointed to the group of winos gathered on the street, "make sure Stephon gets out. And stays out. Or else he'll end up right here, drinkin' with us."

CHAPTER 31

No More Pain

Stanely was a man of his word. A few days later, BTW's yellow school bus lurched down a pothole-ridden street headed to Memphis Academy of Health Sciences High School. Street repair funding was slashed in last year's city budget, and driving in some parts of Memphis could be treacherous, even for big lumbering buses.

"Damn, bruh driving like we five minutes late to tipoff," Tavon griped as his iPhone skidded across the floor under Lenny's seat.

Without missing a beat, Lenny picked it up and passed it back to Terrence behind him. "Tavon, I done told you about all that cursing," barked Lenny.

Joe, the bus driver, stared at Tavon through his rearview mirror. When Tavon got his phone back, the driver purposely ran over a deep pothole in the road, causing Tavon to fall out of his seat and drop his phone again.

"Shit!"

"Tavon!" screamed Lenny. "That's 10 suicides when we get back from this game!" Lenny turned around and put all ten fingers up.

Tavon pulled himself off the ground and shook his head in frustration. The bus driver smiled and winked at Tavon through the rearview mirror. Tavon flashed his middle finger.

Stephon, seated a few rows up from Tavon, bobbed his head to 2Pac's "No More Pain." Terrence leaned over from his seat and unplugged one of Stephon's EarPods, listening closely to the song.

"Bro, didn't this shit come out before we were even born?" Terrence whispered, trying to avoid Lenny's wrath.

Stephon snatched his EarPod back. "My pops had me bump this before every game."

Terrence backed off and slapped his own chest with an open hand apologetically. "My bad, bruh."

"Plus, I'd bump this over *that* any day," Stephon retorted.

The two exchanged smiles.

"Did I just hear somebody disrespect the GOAT?" DaRon inquired as he turned around in his seat and faced Stephon.

Stephon shook his head and looked out the window. Almost simultaneously, he heard the lyrics to "Let's Go" by Key Glock rattle from DaRon's portable Bluetooth speaker.

Almost everyone on the bus began reciting the lyrics, even Lenny. Stephon stood up, looked around the bus, and then pointed to DaRon's speaker.

"See, this why we ain't winning state!" he yelled.

Everyone laughed. Suddenly, the bus stopped, causing Stephon to lunge forward in his seat. "Coach, looks like we got a situation outside," Joe pointed out.

Everyone on the bus scooted to the window. Outside, six police cars with flashing lights were blocking the street. Police officers were pointing their guns at a tinted car with several teenage boys inside.

"Aye, Steph, aren't those the boys from the Frayser game?" asked Terrence.

Stephon moved to the other side of the bus where he could see the action. He watched as the police ordered Smoke and Q out of the car, one by one. Q was in the driver's seat, and Smoke got out of the passenger side. Officers were patting them both down against the car with their hands behind their heads.

"Yep, that's them," Stephon mumbled under his breath.

One of the officers went to the trunk and opened it. The players watched as he shuffled something around before pausing suddenly. Then he raised an assault rifle and a handgun from the trunk, showing both to his partner.

"Oh shit, you see this?" Tavon exclaimed.

Lenny and Tim stared out of the window in shock. A white officer in his twenties directed the bus driver through the police barricade. The bus driver rolled his window down.

"What's going on, officer?"

"Got an anonymous tip about a stolen car in the neighborhood with firearms in the trunk. These boys won't be coming home anytime soon."

Relief washed over Stephon.

Lenny leaned back, letting out a breath he hadn't realized he'd been holding. *Maybe the streets did still have a code, after all.* "Joe, get us outta here," Lenny commanded.

CHAPTER 32

GAME 8

District implications loomed larger than anyone expected and MLK was in a dog fight. "Damn," Lenny groaned. Another miss by Tavon. He was struggling through a cold shooting night. Lenny paced the sidelines, his hands clasped behind his back.

"Back on defense, hustle," Tim shouted from his seat.

Memphis Academy of Health Sciences was refusing to die quietly. MAHS had no business hanging with MLK—their record screamed mediocrity—but here they were, clinging to a four-point lead with minutes bleeding off the clock.

Da'Mon Smith was the reason why. The 6-foot senior moved like liquid lightning, his gleaming bald head cutting through defenders as his killer first step left ankles broken in his wake. A nagging injury had stolen most of his season, but you'd never know it watching him orchestrate this upset. Hampton University had already locked him up with a letter of intent, and tonight he was showing them why.

Every possession felt like borrowed time for MAHS. Every basket from Smith twisted the knife deeper into MLK's playoff dreams. The gym buzzed with nervous energy—upset alerts spreading through the crowd like wildfire.

Smith had the ball again, that familiar crouch signaling another attack. Four points might as well have been forty if they couldn't find an answer for his magic.

Smith brought the ball up court in a hurry. He lost Terrance with a nasty crossover and pulled up at the free throw line for an open jumper. Buckets. Twenty-four points and counting for Smith. The crowd cheered loudly. MAHS's lead increased to six. Two minutes left.

Lenny looked down the bench. Stephon's eyes were already on him. "You ready?" Stephon nodded, hopped up, and ran over to Lenny. "You've got four fouls. This may go to overtime. Play smart. Finish this damn game. It's your time."

Stephon nodded in understanding and checked in at the scorer's table. The horn blared for substitutions, and he entered the game to applause. Even at away games, people were cheering for Stephon. He was making a name for himself around Memphis, with whispers that he could be one of the greats: T-Head, Joe Jackson, Penny, Thaddeus, Keith Lee. Stephon met Tavon at midcourt, and they exchanged fist bumps.

"I'm brick squad tonight," Tavon muttered, frowning hard. "Ready to cook?" Stephon nodded with a smile. "Let's get this dub and go home." Tavon lightly punched Stephon in the chest.

DaRon inbounded the ball to Tavon, who brought it up court. He found Stephon in the corner, but he was quickly double-teamed and threw it back to Tavon. DaRon slashed to the basket, and Tavon lobbed a pass to him for an easy two-hand dunk. The lead was cut to four.

After a miss by MAHS, Tavon hurried up the floor. He rocketed a pass to Stephon in the post, and Stephon flipped in an easy hook. The lead was cut to two.

Lenny eyed the clock. A minute left. He fought the urge to call a timeout. Adversity is your friend—one of Coach Heard's favorites. "Dig deep," Lenny yelled. "Dig deep!"

Smith got by Tavon and was fouled by Terrance while driving to the lane. After he made one of two free throws, MAHS called timeout.

Lenny gathered the team in the huddle. No clipboard. No plays. Just passion. "Three-point game. I'm not leaving here a loser. We got this."

The buzzer sounded. Terrance hustled to the baseline. The referee handed him the ball and blew the whistle. MAHS went into a full-court press for the last possession. Lenny smiled. Big mistake.

Tavon sliced through the chaos, hands flashing for the ball. Terrence threaded it to him through traffic, and Tavon exploded up court like he'd been shot from a cannon. The press crumbled behind him.

DaRon streaked down the sideline, and Tavon's bounce pass hit him in perfect stride. The defense had overcommitted at half-court, leaving the backside wide open. DaRon took two hard dribbles before whipping a cross-court laser to Stephon, who stood alone beyond the arc with his hands already up.

The catch was clean. Stephon squared his shoulders, muscles coiled for the release. A desperate defender charged at him, feet scrambling on the polished hardwood. Too fast. Too frantic. His legs tangled beneath him as he lunged, fingers clawing at Stephon's ankle just as the ball left his hands.

The shot arced through the air, spinning perfect rotation against the lights. Lenny's fist shot skyward before the ball even kissed the net.

Swish.

Then the whistle's sharp blast cut through the celebration. The referee's arm pointed at the fallen defender. Foul. Four-point play opportunity.

The gym erupted.

The home crowd booed the call. MAHS's coach stomped his feet and threw his clipboard to the floor. With only three seconds to play, this was for the win. Stephon went to the free throw line and wiped his hands on his jersey. He looked relaxed. Stephon's mood didn't change during the game. The ref handed him the ball. Stephon inhaled and exhaled deeply. "Take your time son" his father's voice calling from beyond. He shot the free throw. Nothing but net.

MAHS rushed to inbound the ball to Smith, but Terrance and Tavon blanketed him. In desperation, he heaved a near full-court shot that barely missed.

"Game," Lenny howled.

CHAPTER 33

Old Friends

It was almost 11 PM, and Lenny sat alone at the bar. Happy hour had come and gone, and the crowd had thinned out at Sunnybrook. Lenny and Tim had dropped in for a quick dinner of hot wings, fries, and game planning. Tim left around eight o'clock, but Lenny decided to stick around. Ty was bartending, and the drinks were strong.

As Ty poured Lenny another drink, a TV showing SportsCenter displayed Breaking News:

"In sports, a former local hoops star is returning home," said a burly middle-aged anchorman. "Zo Bell was an All-American at Briershire Christian School before going on to star at the University of Tennessee. He was drafted in the first round by the Detroit Pistons and was selected as an NBA All-Star in his 5th season. Bell played for the Atlanta Hawks the past two seasons, but as of tonight, he's been traded to the Memphis Grizzlies. He's expected to join the team later this week."

"Well, I'll be damned," Cliff declared. He turned to Lenny. "My boy is coming home. Let's have that drink."

THE NEXT DAY, while Lenny and Tim were leaving practice, a throng of students was gathered around a matte black Audi R8 with 20-inch Forgiato rims.

"Nice whip," Tim remarked. "Whose car is that?"

They continued walking toward the crowd. The doors opened, and Kendrick Lamar's "Not Like Us" poured out of the car. Zo stepped out, dressed in a Wales Bonner tracksuit and Jordan 1 Off-Whites. A heavy, solid gold Cuban link chain hung from his neck, and diamond stud earrings shone brightly from each ear. A long-legged, caramel-skinned woman ascended from the passenger seat. Nearly six feet tall with spiky blonde hair and Hollywood beauty, she captured just as much attention as Zo.

"Is that Zo?" Tim asked. "That's Zo!" Tim's face lit up. He slapped Lenny on the back and hurried over to join the crowd.

Zo took photos with the students and signed autographs. Lenny plodded over, trying to remember the last time he had seen Zo.

It was eight years ago, during NBA All-Star weekend in New York City. Zo was voted to his first and only All-Star game and flew Lenny in from Italy, where he was playing with Air Avellino.

They spent three nights partying at the best nightclubs, drinking the best liquor, and eating the best food. Everywhere they went, VIP treatment awaited. Back then, the NBA was still a dream for Lenny. He had played in the summer league and had tryouts with the Grizzlies, Hawks, and Mavericks. He felt as though each tryout was one step closer to the NBA, to fulfilling his destiny. All-Star weekend was supposed to be a preview—a glimpse into what his life was to become. In reality, that night was as close as he ever got.

"Chase Money," Zo yelled over the crowd. Lenny nodded and snaked his way through the crowd. He and Zo embraced. "Been too long, my guy, been too long."

"Whatchu doing around these parts, big-time? Shouldn't you be at a press conference or something?"

"Nah man, your guy A.J. got it pushed back for me. Said you was coaching now. Can't lie—I didn't believe him. Always figured I'd retire before you."

Zo's grin lingered, but his eyes scanned Lenny's face like he was trying to read a headline that wasn't there.

Lenny tried to hide his shame with a disingenuous smile. "I got tired of living halfway across the world. And as much as I love me some baklava and kofta, ain't nothing like a rack of ribs."

Zo laughed. "Come through Vibes tomorrow and celebrate whicha boy. And bring one of your chicks with you; I know you got plenty." Zo chuckled again.

"Appreciate it, bro. I'll try to make it out."

Stephon, Tavon, and DaRon came outside of the gym as Zo walked back to his Audi. The three of them walked up behind Lenny.

"Coach, who was that?" Stephon asked.

"Damn, that nigga clean as hell in the Audi," Tavon chimed in.

"Watch your mouth, Tavon." Lenny commanded. "That's Zo Bell."

"Zo Bell who plays for the Grizzlies now?!" DaRon yelled.

DaRon and Tavon sprinted toward Zo's Audi, trying to grab his autograph before he climbed into his car.

Stephon stayed behind, his heart racing like his teammates. But something about Lenny's sullen demeanor made him stay behind. "You good, coach?"

Lenny unfolded his arms and changed his tight facial expression. "Yeah, I'm good." Lenny walked toward his car and opened the driver's side door. He pointed at Zo. "One day, that'll be you."

"I sure hope so," Stephon whispered to himself.

CHAPTER 34

Homecoming

Lenny woke up the next day groggy from a sleepless night. He headed into the kitchen, where his mother was pulling a quiche out of the oven. Eddie sat at the kitchen island, drinking coffee and reading the sports section of The Commercial Appeal. Bill Withers' "Lovely Day" played from the Echo.

"Morning," Eddie said, holding up the newspaper. "Hear the news about Zo Bell?"

Lenny opened the fridge door and pulled out a carafe of freshly squeezed orange juice. "Yeah, I heard."

Patricia wiped her hands on her apron and handed Lenny a glass. He filled the glass with juice. "Alonzo Bell?" Patricia asked.

"Yes, the NBA player," Eddie replied. "He was traded to the Grizzlies. He's coming back home."

"Wow." Patricia refilled her coffee mug. "I haven't heard that name in years. He and Lenny were best friends growing up. Practically inseparable." She sat next to Eddie at the island. "Quiche is cooling down."

Eddie glanced at Lenny's empty facial expression and could sense something was off.

Lenny leaned against the sink. "He stopped by MLK yesterday with some chick. Says he wants to hang out at the club tomorrow. We'll see."

"We'll see?" Patricia questioned, head jerking back slightly. "You two are best friends."

"We were best friends," Lenny corrected. "We really haven't talked in years."

Patricia went to the counter and began slicing the quiche. "Well, maybe this is fate that he's back in Memphis."

Lenny sat down opposite Eddie at the island. "Yeah, maybe."

Eddie folded the newspaper. "None of my business, Lenny, but I know a few things. And there is no friend like an old friend."

Patricia set two plates of quiche down on the island. "I concur. Now let's eat before this quiche gets cold."

CHAPTER 35

Shelby Farms

Lenny loved his Saturday morning jogs at Shelby Farms. Four thousand acres of wilderness stretched from Memphis to Cordova. It was dirt trails, glassy lakes, geese skimming across the water. No sirens. No loud noises. No fear. It brought Lenny calm.

Every run returned him to boyhood. Huffing up hills with Zo and Cliff on weekends, weight vests strapped tight, lungs burning. Cliff barking at them to quit being soft, threatening to run them til they puked.

Lenny was always faster, but sometimes he'd slow just enough to let Zo close the gap — spare him the quiet car rides home where Cliff would berate him for coming in second.

He propped one foot on a park bench and leaned into the stretch, trying to ignore the biting pain in his knee. Earbuds jammed deep, J. Cole's "Love Yourz" vibrated through his body.

Then he was off, settling into the rhythm of the dirt beneath his soles. The trail wound five miles through rustling leaves and cool air that scraped his lungs clean.

His mind bounced from one worry to the next: replaying the win over MAHS, marveling at Stephon's raw brilliance, quietly thanking Stanley for keeping his promise. Things were clicking. For the first time in a long stretch, peace didn't feel so far off. His morning runs outnumbered his nights at Sunnybrook now. Game plans with Stats and Tim took the place of slow drags and cheap whiskey with Jamel.

Five miles disappeared too quickly. He glanced at his watch and grinned—new record. He slowed to a walk, heart thundering less violently. His knee still pulsed, but it was manageable. He wiped sweat from his brow and let himself feel good, just for a beat.

Then a familiar shape appeared up ahead. Long, athletic legs in black spandex. 1867 stitched bold across the back of a tee, a bison under it—repping Howard University. Natural curls bursting from the slit in her baseball cap. It was Katrina. Body still tight like high school, still the most in-shape woman he'd ever known.

What were the odds? Today was the day he decided. All those words he'd swallowed at Sunnybrook—he'd finally let them out. He quickened his step, closing the gap to forty yards—then, stopped cold.

Zo's unmistakable, lanky silhouette emerged. That easy 6'9" glide. Lenny watched him close the space to Katrina, lean down, and wrap her up in one of those long-armed hugs that used to belong to Lenny. His stomach folded into knots so tight it felt like he might vomit.

They took off jogging side by side, ponytail bouncing, Zo's long strides matching hers. Two silhouettes shrunk into the trees, leaving him stranded on the trail with a thousand cuts inside him.

How long had this been going on? Who knew about it? Were they laughing behind his back all these years—or worse, tiptoeing around him, swallowing truths out of pity?

The questions battered him in relentless waves. He finally reached his car and collapsed into the driver's seat. He gripped the steering wheel until his knuckles ached.

He stared at the cracked windshield for a long time. Then pulled out his phone and shot off a text to Tim.

Practice tomorrow. Make sure everybody's there.

Tim responded almost immediately.

👀 *Thought Sundays were for rest.*

Lenny took a long pull from the flask hidden in his console, wiped his mouth. He didn't even feel the burn. He was numb again.

9am Tim. Have their asses there.

CHAPTER 36

Lucky

Sunday morning, somehow, Tim was able to secure each player's attendance at practice. No church; no rest this Sunday. Lenny paced the sidelines sweating as profusely as his players, a mixture of anger and alcohol bubbling to the surface.

"Tavon, how many times do I have to tell you to pass the damn ball?" Lenny blew the whistle feverishly. "This practice has been pitiful. Northside is going to kick our asses on Monday."

"Coach, no one was open." Tavon shrugged his shoulders. "The play doesn't work."

"Everybody on the baseline!" Lenny blew his whistle again. The players groaned. "Hurry up, dammit."

Tim stood at the opposite baseline. "Running them every five seconds isn't helping," he mumbled.

"Five suicides!" Lenny blew the whistle, and the first group of players raced up the court. Stephon led the pack with DaRon on his heels. Tavon and Terrence struggled to keep pace.

"Five. Four. Three. Two. One. Start over. Terrence didn't touch the line."

"Lenny, man, we have a game tomorrow. Take it easy," Tim pleaded.

All the players groaned. Stephon stepped toward Lenny. "Coach, Tavon's right. The play doesn't work. The defense just overplays the back cut."

"Raise your hand if you've ever played professional basketball." Lenny raised a hand to his rhetorical question and spun around the gym. "Nobody? Just me? That's what I thought."

"I'm not running anymore," Tavon announced. "Fuck this."

"What did you say?" Lenny stuffed his whistle inside his t-shirt and beelined toward Tavon. Tim rushed toward Lenny, catching up right as he got into Tavon's face.

"Chill, Lenny." Tim stepped in between the two. "He's just talking out his ass."

Stephon pulled Tavon away. "Chill, fool."

Tavon snatched away from Stephon and took off his jersey. He threw the jersey on the ground and walked toward the locker room as the rest of the teammates watched.

"If any of y'all want to join him, feel free." The gym fell silent. "What y'all waiting for? Get back on the line if you still want to be on this team!"

The first group, except for Stephon, prepared to run. Stephon stood still, looking in the direction of the locker room.

"Stephon, you deaf?" Lenny snapped. Stephon looked at Lenny and then walked over to the rest of the group. "Good. You ain't special, son. I've seen better players than you never leave South Memphis."

Tavon walked out of the locker room dressed in a sweatsuit with a backpack slung over his shoulder. He looked at Stephon. "I can't play for this drunk-ass dude anymore, man. I get enough of that shit at home." Everyone except Lenny watched with remorse as he exited the gym.

Lenny shrugged and walked toward center court. "Good riddance. Y'all are lucky to be on this team."

"We're not lucky; you are," Stephon shouted, fuming.

Lenny whipped around and glared at Stephon. "What did you say?"

Everyone in the gym turned to Stephon. "I said, you're the lucky one. Lucky we don't go to Davenport about your drinking before every game. Lucky we come to practice every day for a coach who can't even remember his own plays. Lucky we let you take your failures out on us."

A tense moment of silence followed before Lenny ordered, "Get out of my gym!"

Stephon took his jersey off and threw it on the floor before heading to the locker room. As Stephon disappeared from sight, Lenny blew the whistle for the first group to start running, but no one moved.

Terrence pulled off his jersey and tossed it to the ground. DaRon followed suit. Within seconds, practice jerseys were strewn all over the gym floor. Tim shook his head and took a seat at the scorer's table.

Stats unplugged the score clock and closed his laptop. "Looks like we won't be needing any of this for a while."

Tim turned to Stats, shaking his head in disappointment. "I think you might be right."

CHAPTER 37

Choices

L enny stomped on the gas, nodding to Project Pat's "Choices."
Jamel carefully rolled a blunt in the passenger seat. "Crank that
up!"

The volume rose to a deafening level, shaking the car. Lenny
and Jamel both rapped along with the lyrics. Lenny took a swig from
a red plastic cup. "Fill me up." Jamel lifted the bottle of Remy
Martin nudged between his feet and filled Lenny's cup.

"Mane, it's good to get away from this coaching shit for a change.
These kids just don't know how much work goes into making the
league."

Looking in his rearview mirror, Lenny spotted a police cruiser
behind him, lights flashing and siren blaring. "Shit. 12. Put that
weed away."

Jamel stuffed the bag of weed and blunt down the front of his
pants. "What should I do? I've been drinking."

Jamel shrugged. "Pull over, man. Don't say shit; you'll be
straight."

Lenny pulled over. He finished the last of his cup. "Shit." He
pulled out his license and put it on the dashboard.

Later that evening, Lenny sat in a large holding cell that smelled
of piss, body odor, and commercial disinfectant. Two bald Hispanic
gangbangers with face tattoos argued in Spanish. A junkie sat on the

cement floor, arms wrapped around his knees, rocking back and forth and humming a children's song. An obese man with a shaggy mullet in overalls and no shirt held his bleeding hand and grunted heavily every thirty seconds.

Eddie was led by an officer to the holding area. He stood outside the cell door.

The officer looked at Eddie quizzically. "This him?"

Eddie nodded. The officer unlocked the cell door, Eddie walked in, and the officer locked the door behind him. Everyone in the cell looked up. Eddie sat down next to Lenny.

"Jamel called me. And don't worry, I didn't tell your mother."

"Thanks, Eddie. I fucked up. For real this time." Lenny shook his head ruefully. He wiped a tear from his eye. "The school is going to find out. I'll probably get fired. Coach Heard would be ashamed." Lenny slammed his fist down on the bench.

"What's behind you doesn't matter. You can only focus on what lies ahead."

"And what if you don't like where you're headed?"

"Then you got a choice to make. Keep down that path or turn around and find another way."

Lenny dropped his head and nodded in agreement. Eddie put his arm around his shoulder.

"But only a sober mind can make the right choices."

Eddie patted Lenny on the back and guided him toward the exit. "Let's go, Coach."

Outside the precinct, Lenny followed Eddie as they got into Eddie's truck. Eddie paused before turning the key in the ignition. "They're going to charge you with reckless driving, not a DUI. I'm still owed a couple of favors around here. I cashed in."

Lenny exhaled deeply. "Thank you, Eddie. Thank you. That's a solid I won't forget. I owe you, BIG TIME."

"You don't owe me; you owe yourself. Choices. Make the right ones from here on out; that's all I ask."

"I will."

Eddie started the engine, and they pulled off.

CHAPTER 38

Dead End

Lenny sat outside Principal Davenport's office, tapping his feet. One of the office administrators, a fleshy older woman with cropped gray hair and horn-rimmed glasses, motioned for Lenny to go in.

Principal Davenport was sitting behind her desk when Lenny entered her office. Without looking up from her computer screen, she eyed Lenny sharply from the corner of her eye. "Close the door and have a seat."

Lenny pushed the door closed behind him and took a seat in one of the chairs in front of her desk. "What's up, Trina? Your text seemed urgent. Everything good?" Lenny asked, his voice slightly cracking.

Principal Davenport turned away from her computer screen, reared back in her chair, and exhaled deeply. "When I took this job, the principal who retired before me gave me a piece of advice that sticks with me til this day." She pointed to a hand-drawn poster on her wall with the words "Put The Kids First."

Lenny shifted his attention toward the poster. "Okay."

"Yesterday, I got a call from one of my student's parents. She's MPD. She says she booked one of our coaches last night on a DUI."

Lenny's face fell. "Listen, Trina, I can explain."

"Don't bother." Principal Davenport leaned forward. "I'm going to talk, and you're going to listen."

Lenny slumped back in his chair and folded his arms with pursed lips. Principal Davenport reached into her drawer and pulled out a stack of files. She selected one from the pile.

"Tavon Graham. Grade point average: 2.5. Suspended three times in the 9th grade for cutting class. His mother works three jobs. His drunk father just got out of jail for breaking her nose during a domestic violence dispute. His mother can't afford to send him to college; basketball is his only chance."

Principal Davenport tossed Tavon's file to the side and picked up another. "DaRon Scott. Lives in a trailer park with his mother, who is a known addict. His father was killed by police when he was 7. ACT score: 21. He sleeps in most of his classes because he works overnight to help his mom pay the bills."

"I get it." Lenny sat up, trying to interject.

Principal Davenport raised her hand in protest. "I'm not done."

She picked up another file and raised it in Lenny's direction. "Terrence Price, 3.8 GPA. 32 on the ACT. Honors society. He'll be the first person in his family to attend college. His mother died from breast cancer two years ago. His father drives trucks to pay the bills. Terrence takes care of his younger brother and sister while their father is away."

"Let's see," she continued. "Shawn Woodson, aka Stats. Suffers from muscular dystrophy—a genetic disorder that weakens the body's muscles. He's been in a wheelchair since the age of ten and almost committed suicide a few years ago due to depression."

Principal Davenport held the entire stack of files in the air. "Should I continue?"

Lenny could only shake his head.

Principal Davenport paused before continuing. "Did you even attempt to get to know these young men off the court and try to understand what they're going through? Or were you too caught up in your own self-pity to consider anyone's feelings but your own?"

Lenny looked down into his lap as if searching for words but found none.

Principal Davenport shook her head and sighed. "I didn't think so. I'm guessing that's why the entire team quit yesterday." She inhaled deeply and exhaled slowly. She stood up from her chair and walked to the window.

"These kids need more than a basketball coach. They need guidance. Hope. Consistency. They need someone to believe in and someone who believes in them. You played for Coach Heard; I figured you knew this."

Lenny thought of Tavon's face when he stormed out, of Stephon's eyes—that mix of fury and disappointment that cut deeper than anything Zo or Katrina ever did. Lenny stood up. "Listen, I'm sorry. I messed up. We all mess up."

Principal Davenport turned to face Lenny. "You've got one day to clean out your office. Tim will coach the team for the remainder of the season."

Lenny's shoulders stiffened. "What?!"

He walked a few steps toward Principal Davenport. "I deserve at least one more chance," he pleaded, his hands clasped together before him.

Principal Davenport sat back down at her desk, picked up the phone, and began dialing a number. "Close the door on your way out."

Lenny opened his mouth to speak but instead huffed out of the room, slamming the door behind him.

CHAPTER 39

GAME 20

Tim paced the sideline. "Front the post, DaRon," he yelled. Almost as if on cue, Northside's point guard dribbled to the left wing and whipped a bounce pass around Stephon's outstretched arms and legs. DaRon was sealed behind Northside's big man, Angel Walker, a 6'9", 230-pound brick wall. Walker caught the ball, made a quick drop-step move to the basket that knocked DaRon to the floor, and tomahawk dunked the ball. Walker roared in celebration and stared DaRon down afterward.

DaRon gathered himself and inbounded the ball to Tavon. Twenty seconds remained until halftime, and Northside held an eight-point lead.

"Tavon, run Memphis," Tim shouted from the sideline as Tavon stepped past half court.

Tavon ignored the play call and raised a fist in the air, signaling Terrence to set a pick at the top of the key. Stephon watched from the strong side corner with his knees slightly bent and hands open, in shooting position.

Tavon sold the defender with a subtle hesitation, then knifed toward the rim. Bodies collapsed on him like a vice—exactly what he wanted. In his peripheral vision, Stephon had drifted to the corner, forgotten and alone.

The pass came hot and low. Stephon's hands were ready, muscle memory taking over as he squared his feet and elevated in one fluid motion. The ball climbed toward the rafters, rotation perfect, arc climbing high above the outstretched fingers of a late-closing defender.

Time suspended. The buzzer's wail cut through the gym just as leather kissed net.

Swish.

Northside 55, MLK 50 at the break.

Tavon pumped his fist as both teams jogged toward their respective locker rooms, the shot's echo still hanging in the air. Tim trailed behind his teammates, scratching his head in bewilderment. They'd played nearly perfect basketball for twenty minutes, and somehow, they were still losing.

The taste of that shot would linger in everyone's mouth during halftime—sweet for one side, bitter for the other.

The horn sounded to start the second half. As Tim walked back to the bench, he spotted Lenny sitting alone near the top of the bleachers, disguised in a black hoodie and hat. The two shared a head nod.

As the third quarter wound down, MLK's turnovers and poor shooting helped Northside take a commanding lead heading into the final period. During the break between the third and fourth quarters, the team sat on the bench dejected. Tim looked up at the scoreboard with disappointment.

Stats broke the silence from his wheelchair seated behind the bench. "Down fifteen points to this team. We're better than this."

Tavon took a sip of Gatorade and looked over at Stats. "Last time I checked, the scoreboard doesn't lie."

Tim looked up at Lenny and shrugged. Lenny removed his hoodie and made an X symbol from the bleachers. Tim nodded in understanding and smiled.

"Everybody listen up," Tim demanded. "We're going to press these guys full court for the entire fourth quarter."

There was a collective groan from the team. Tim looked the players in their eyes. "Trust me. Terrence, you're on the ball. Use your long arms to block the inbounds passer's vision. Stephon and DaRon, I want you both at the front of the press. Harrison and Tavon, stay in the back."

Stats smiled and nodded in agreement. "They won't be able to see over the press, which means long passes for steals."

Tim smiled. "That's right, and when they make the big man the passer, I want to trap the first pass hard and let them give it back to him and dare him to dribble. Hands in." The team placed their fists in the center circle.

"Defense on three. One. Two. Three."

"DEFENSE," the entire team chanted.

Terrence, Stephon, and DaRon set up the front of the press to begin the quarter. On the very first play, Northside attempted a long baseball pass to Angel Walker, but Tavon was watching the play unfold like a free safety watching a quarterback's eyes. He leapt into the passing lane and intercepted the ball. Northside scrambled to defend, but Tavon found DaRon near the basket for an easy dunk.

Northside's coach signaled for Angel to take the ball out. Angel passed the ball to Northside's point guard in the corner. DaRon and Stephon immediately converged and trapped him. Northside's point guard panicked and quickly passed back to Angel but overthrew him. Turnover, MLK's ball.

DaRon slapped the ball with his hand and watched the inbounds play develop. Stephon flashed open and received a pass on the wing, closely guarded. He pump-faked and baited his defender into the air. While the Northside defender was airborne, Stephon raised up for a jumper and lunged into his defender to draw a foul. The whistle blew as Stephon's wild shot attempt somehow struck the perfect spot on the backboard and fell into the basket. Tim pumped his fist with vigor from the sideline as the team huddled together before Stephon's free throw shot. Swish. 75-67 Northside. Timeout.

The team sprinted to the sidelines to greet Tim with newfound swagger.

"Listen, we still have a long way to go." Tim glanced at the scoreboard anxiously.

"They're taking the big man out and putting in 40," Stats observed. "He shoots 35% from the free-throw line."

Tim rubbed his chin in thought. "Ricky, go in for Tavon."

"What?!" Tavon snapped.

Stephon attempted to calm Tavon. "Just for defense."

"Exactly," Tim agreed. "You have four fouls."

Tim's hack-a-Shaq gamble was paying dividends. Number 40 — a rail-thin kid whose goggles made him look more like a lab assistant than a basketball player—stepped to the line and clanked the front end of the one-and-one off the back iron.

Stephon snatched the rebound and ignited the break, weaving through traffic like he was born for this moment. Past half-court, through the lane, until he hit the free-throw line and suddenly the gym understood what was coming.

He launched himself skyward, rising over a 6'4" Northside defender who looked tiny beneath Stephon's shadow. The dunk came down like thunder—a ferocious, rim-rattling slam that sent shockwaves through the building. Even the Northside faithful couldn't help themselves. They rose to their feet, swept up in the beauty of athletic poetry. The gym exploded in reluctant appreciation for greatness.

But when the roar died, only one person wasn't celebrating. Stephon lay crumpled beneath the basket, clutching his ankle, his face twisted in agony that had nothing to do with the score. The moment of triumph had turned to nightmare in the span of a heartbeat.

Tavon and DaRon were there before the echo faded, dropping to their knees beside their fallen star.

Tavon offered his hand to Stephon. "Aye, you good?"

"Don't move him," Lenny ordered as he rushed over. Tim stood next to him. "Can you move it?"

Stephon grimaced in pain but nodded yes.

"Good, it's probably not a break." Lenny extended his hand to Stephon. "We're going to help you stand up and see if you can put pressure on it."

A referee walked over. "Coach, if he can't shoot the free throw, he's done for the night."

"I'm good," Stephon pushed himself up. "I can stay in."

Lenny faced Tim. "Take him out. It's too risky."

Stephon stood up straight. "I'm fine."

Tim looked from Lenny to Stephon. "Knock down the free throws." Lenny shook his head in disapproval and returned to the bleachers.

Both free throws found their mark. Northside 75, MLK 70. One minute left—an eternity and a heartbeat all at once.

Tim barked orders, his voice cutting through the crowd noise as his team dropped into zone coverage. Stephon hobbled back on defense, each step a reminder of battles fought. Angel had returned to exploit the obvious weakness—Stephon's battered body—and Northside's coach was already pointing toward the post, sensing blood in the water.

The entry pass came soft and perfect. Angel caught it low, backing down Stephon with the methodical power of a bulldozer. Stephon planted his feet and tried to hold ground, but his legs betrayed him. Angel spun toward the rim, layup all but guaranteed.

Then DaRon appeared like a ghost from the weak side, timing his leap perfectly. His hand met ball against glass with a thunderous *crack* that sent the crowd into delirium.

Harrison scooped the loose ball and fired a baseball pass to Tavon, who had already turned and sprinted toward the other end. Alone. Uncontested. A sure two points to cut the lead to one.

Instead, Tavon pulled up behind the arc and let it fly.

Hero or fool—the line was thinner than the net he was aiming for.

"Tavon, nooooo!" yelled Tim.

Lenny stood with his hands up in disbelief. The ball touched every part of the rim and fell into the hoop. 75-73 Northside. Tavon did an imitation bow-and-arrow shot toward a Northside defender and then turned and winked at Tim. Stephon and Tavon high-fived each other at half court. 30 seconds remained.

Northside's point guard attempted to dribble out the clock. He stayed low in a protective dribble with his back to Tavon, who sat just as low, searching for an opening. 15 seconds remained.

"Foul," shouted Tim.

The Northside point guard picked up his dribble at half-court, expecting the foul that never came. He didn't see DaRon streaking from his blind side until it was too late. The trap closed like jaws, forcing him off balance, stumbling backwards as precious seconds bled away.

His desperation heave hung in the air like a prayer nobody believed in. Harrison read it perfectly, snatching the pass and exploding toward the other end. The crowd rose as one, sensing something magical brewing.

Five seconds on the clock when Harrison crossed the three-point line. Four seconds when he launched the ball skyward—a rainbow arcing toward the rim that could have been anything: shot, pass, or pure instinct.

Three seconds. Two seconds.

Stephon materialized beneath the basket like he'd been summoned, rising to meet the ball at its peak. Angel Walker jumped with him, but Stephon hung in the air longer, impossibly suspended as the horn began its wail. The dunk came down like judgment, rattling the rim and silencing the building for one perfect heartbeat.

Then chaos. The gym exploded as players and fans realized what they'd witnessed. 75-75.

The whistle cut through the celebration like a blade. Foul. Angel's desperate swipe had caught Stephon's arm.

One free throw for the lead.

The referee held the ball. "One shot. Everybody off the line."

Stephon hobbled toward the free-throw line. His teammates watched anxiously from the sidelines. Tim paced back and forth. The roar in the gym was deafening as Northside fans screamed. Stephon took a deep breath and briefly closed his eyes. He envisioned shooting free throws at the park with his father and could hear his father's voice: One more, and we're done for the day, Steph. Stephon bent his knees and followed through toward the rim, leaving his wrist pointed to the ground. 76-75 MLK.

The team rushed the floor and lifted Stephon into the air as he smiled and grimaced at the same time. Tim and Stats shared an emotional hug. As the celebration subsided and the team lined up to shake hands with the Northside players and coaches. Stephon limped off the court, alone for a moment, searching the rafters. But Lenny was gone. Again.

CHAPTER 40

The Price of Greatness

Stephon sat up in bed, one leg propped atop a pillow, an ice pack wrapped lightly around his swollen ankle. He scrolled through Instagram. Highlights of the Northside game had already made their way to his feed.

Tavon's story featured a boomerang video clip of Stephon dunking over Angel Walker, with airplane emojis in the foreground. Stephon laughed. As he continued scrolling, he watched DaRon's live feed, which showed their post-game celebration. Stephon smiled and then received a notification on his phone.

[Sadat wants to play chess]

[MLKFinest has entered the chatroom]

Sadat: You've been dodging me lately. When's my rematch?

MLKFinest: My bad. School and ball been keeping me busy.

Sadat: How's the season?

MLKFinest: Made the city championship for the first time in 10 years.

Sadat: Nice! Sounds like that new coach over there knows what he's doing. [white rook from H3 to F3]

MLKFinest: He's not our coach anymore. [black pawn from E7 to E5].

Sadat: What happened?

MLKFinest: He was drunk all the time, yelling at us; we got sick of his shit. So, we walked out on him.

Sadat: [white knight from B1 to C3] LOL

MLKFinest: What's funny?

Sadat: Your coach sounds like me 10 years ago.

MLKFinest: [black bishop from F8 to D6] Whatchu mean?

Sadat: I wanted my son to be the next Maurice Ashley. Pushed him every day. He wasn't natural like you, but he worked hard. Work ethic that I rarely gave him credit for.

MLKFinest: I didn't know you have a son.

Sadat: A son, a wife. But I guess they got sick of my shit too. Packed up and moved to Atlanta 8 years ago. Ain't seen them since. My son became a grandmaster at 20 years old. I never saw any of his matches. [white rook from A2 to A4]

MLKFinest: Damn. Why didn't you just beg them to come back? Tell them you'd changed.

Sadat: I missed my chance. Too much pride. See, I was taught that being great requires sacrifice, even if that meant sacrificing my own family. I know now that no amount of greatness is worth losing the people you love. But it took me losing them to learn that. I'm not sure what that coach of yours is going through, but it sounds like he just lost the best thing he had going for him.

MLKFinest: [black knight from B8 to C6] I gotta go, Sadat. Let's finish this game later.

[MLKFinest exits chat room and game]

Stephon put his phone down. He thought about Sadat and what he revealed. He picked his phone up and reread the texts. Stephon hobbled over and flipped off the light switch. He got back into bed and silently stared at the ceiling. "Everyone deserves a chance at redemption" His father would tell him. His eyes were half-closed when he received a text from.

Stats: Aye, check out the Commercial Appeal article from last night's game. [link]

Stephon opened the link and read the article with a wide smile. He placed his hands behind his head and continued staring at the ceiling until he fell asleep.

CHAPTER 41

Everyone Has a Mountain to Climb

A diverse group of blue-collar men and women milled about the musty, dimly lit East Memphis Presbyterian church basement. In the center of the room, beige metal folding chairs formed a large circle. On a white folding banquet table against the wall sat assorted packaged snacks and a pot of coffee. Lenny nervously followed Eddie into the low-ceiling room.

A gangly bearded man wearing an old Army fatigue jacket and a frayed ball cap with USS CONSTELLATION etched in bold letters across the front approached Eddie with a crooked smile. "Gotdamn, I'm seeing a ghost."

Eddie returned the smile. "Downey, it's been a minute."

"I'll say." The two shared a friendly handshake. "Should I be happy or sad that you're here?"

"Twenty years sober and counting."

Downey breathed a sigh of relief. "Amen, brother, amen."

Eddie rested his hand on Lenny's shoulder. "This is my friend Lenny."

Downey extended his hand. Lenny shook it. "Nice to meet you, Lenny. A friend of Eddie's is a friend of mine."

"Downey and I worked together in homicide for a few years," Eddie added.

"Eddie is the best damn cop I ever worked with, scout's honor." Downey crossed his chest.

"Well, I wouldn't go that far, or maybe I would." Eddie and Downey shared a laugh. "Downey got me sober. He helped me climb the mountain and not fall off."

Downey laid a hand on Eddie's shoulder. "It's not the mountain we conquer, but ourselves." Eddie nodded in recognition. Downey looked at Lenny. "Everyone has a mountain to climb. Remember that." Eddie lightly tapped Lenny on the shoulder and made his way into the middle of the circle of chairs. "Folks, grab your snacks and coffee so we can begin," Downey said loudly.

Eddie and Lenny sat down. Lenny leaned over to Eddie. "I'm not sure about this. AA?"

"Remember what I said about choices."

Lenny nodded, unconvinced. He watched as people took their seats, filling up the circle. After everyone was seated, Downey took his seat in the middle of the circle and removed his hat.

Lenny and Eddie sat across from each other in Muddy's Bake Shop. Lenny picked at a slice of Prozac cake. Eddie finished eating his slice and quickly started working on a second slice.

"Your mother would kill me if she saw me right now," Eddie joked. "She's always on me about my sugar intake. I just love sweets." Eddie grinned and finished the second slice.

Lenny pushed the rest of his slice over to Eddie. "Our secret." Eddie nodded and began eating the rest of Lenny's slice. Lenny leaned back in his chair.

Eddie finished the slice and exhaled deeply. He rubbed his stomach. "Whoo wee. I'm stuffed." They both laughed. Eddie leaned forward, rested his elbows on the table, and clasped his hands together. "I know that was a lot tonight. Your first meeting."

Lenny nodded in agreement and rubbed his palms together. He lowered his voice. "I, I, I never saw myself going to AA."

Eddie nodded. "Me either. I thought I had it under control. But what's under control? I couldn't grapple with that answer. And I was finding myself pushing the boundaries of control too often."

Lenny and Eddie sat in silence. Lenny rubbed the handle of his fork, his eyes fixed on the utensil.

Eddie moved his plates to the side. Lenny looked up from the fork. "Growing up, I was always compared to my brother. He was an all-state running back at Melrose. Football was his thing. I struggled to find my thing. My father used to always say that everyone's alarm clock goes off at different times. At some point, you have to realize that you don't have it under control. That you need help. That you must make the right choices. Downey said it best: Everyone has a mountain to climb."

Lenny nodded with approval, taking it all in.

"Just remember, Len — you don't gotta reach the top today. Just keep climbing."

CHAPTER 42

The Chosen One

Inside his office, Lenny packed his belongings. Old plaques and trophies jutted from a banker's box on the sofa. He stopped and stared at a photo hanging on the wall of him and Coach Heard. His eyes began to water.

"I remember that game. State championship, right?" Principal Davenport said, as she leaned on the door frame.

Lenny turned around; half startled. "I didn't even hear you come in. Just finishing up here; won't be too much longer," Lenny responded as he quickly wiped his eyes.

Principal Davenport rested against the doorway. "You know, the last time I saw Coach Heard before he passed, he was talking about you."

Lenny sat on the corner of his desk. "Oh yeah?" he said, with a disinterested tone.

"I visited him over at Baptist Hospital a few times. The old man could barely remember my name; he called me 'that girl Lenny used to date.'" Principal Davenport chuckled.

Lenny turned away, found an empty banker's box, and began filling it up, avoiding eye contact. Still not completely over seeing her with Zo.

Principal Davenport lowered her voice to sound like Coach Heard. "That Lenny, he... he's gonna be special." She chuckled again. "Even with dementia, he remembered you, Lenny. He loved you like a son."

Lenny took down the photo of him and Coach Heard and dropped it into the box he was holding. "Coach always was too stubborn. Didn't know when to give up on people."

"How are the AA meetings going?"

Lenny fidgeted with the box. "How did you know?" he stammered.

"You know nothing in this city is a secret." Principal Davenport shrugged. "I'm glad to see that you're not giving up on yourself."

Lenny shifted his weight from side to side. "Everyone has a mountain to climb, apparently."

"I can't argue with you there." Principal Davenport stepped into the doorway. "It took ten years for me to climb Mount Everest."

"What's that mean?"

"You never asked me why I don't have any kids."

Lenny shrugged. "None of my business. Plus, you got a thousand kids to watch after every day."

Principal Davenport shook her head. "Every woman wants kids of her own, Lenny. We're wired that way. Unfortunately, my wires got crossed somehow. I'll never have any, not naturally anyway."

Lenny looked at Principal Davenport as she rummaged through his box. "I'm sorry, Katrina. I had no idea."

Principal Davenport sat down on the couch. "It's fine. The news led to depression. The depression led my husband astray. And that led to divorce."

Lenny stopped packing. He sat back down on the edge of his desk.

Principal Davenport continued. "Working here at MLK became my purpose in life. My passion. It replaced the void I felt every time I thought about having a child of my own."

Lenny's face suddenly turned solemn. "Well, at least you have something."

A brief silence ensued. Lenny drummed his fingers on the desk. Suddenly, the sounds of sneakers squeaking against the floor and laughing teenagers broke the silence.

Lenny stood up from the desk, puzzled. "It's Sunday. The gym is closed. What are these kids doing here?"

Principal Davenport smiled at Lenny. "Filling the void." She got up from the couch and walked out of the office. Lenny could hear her conversation but could not see who she was talking to. "Gentlemen, I expect to see all of you on time at school tomorrow."

"Yes, Principal Davenport," the crowd replied in unison.

Seconds later, Stats wheeled into Lenny's office. Next came Terrence. Then DaRon, Tavon, and Harrison. Before long, the entire team was crowded inside Lenny's tiny office. Tim made his way in. Eventually, Stephon pushed through from the back with a newspaper in his hand and placed it on Lenny's desk. He opened it to the sports column. The front page read "MLK IS BACK!"

"Anyone who ever made a mistake in life, raise your hand." Stephon turned and looked around the room. All hands were up. "Everybody makes mistakes, Coach. It's what makes us human. You once told us that our mistakes don't define us; our choices do."

Tavon stepped forward timidly. "We choose you, coach."

Lenny held back tears. Tim stood in the back of the office and smiled. They nodded to each other. Lenny raised the newspaper and thrust it into the air. "MLK is back!" He continued to raise the newspaper high as the group screamed in unison and embraced him.

CHAPTER 43

Know Your Why

Lenny hovered over Coach Heard's tombstone. He whispered a silent prayer before removing two Yoo-hoos from inside his jacket. He placed one atop the headstone and sat down on the grass to open the second Yoo-hoo.

Lenny raised the Yoo-hoo, toasted, "Cheers," and took a sip. "No more liquor. Now, I'm addicted to these. I see why you loved them. They're bussin."

Lenny took another sip. "Been a while," he confessed. "Coaching takes up so much time, but you already know that. You always said coaching is not a profession; it's a calling. You were right."

"We've got a big game tonight. I'm a little nervous. I remember before big games you'd always say to 'know your why'. I understand that now more than ever." Lenny finished the Yoo-Hoo and stood up. "I know you'll be there tonight for MLK, for me. Miss you, coach."

Tim climbed aboard the team bus, followed by Lenny. Tim raised both hands in the air. "Quiet," he shouted.

The bus fell silent. The players, jarred by Tim's tone, turned their attention to the front of the bus.

"Today is a big fucking game," Lenny barked. "Remember your why. When you're tired and feel like quitting, remember why you're here."

All eyes were on Lenny as he paced up and down the bus aisle. "Why did you practice so hard? Why did you miss out on parties? Why did you spend your free time in the gym? Why did you wake up early to work out? Why did you stay up late to shoot extra jumpers? Why?"

The players conveyed understanding with nodding heads. Lenny stood at the front of the bus, hands gripping the seats in front of him. "Think about those questions on the bus ride. I want silence. No talking. At all!"

Lenny and Tim sat down in the front row seats of the bus. They looked at each other and nodded.

CHAPTER 44

Make Your Own Destiny

GAME 29

Manassas High School, in North Memphis, was fighting for a state tournament berth. Like MLK, Manassas struggled early in the season but was riding a four-game winning streak thanks to senior DayMarr Hood, a 6'4" guard with a silky jumper. Arms covered in tattoos, DayMarr had been in and out of the juvenile system a dozen times since he was nine years old. Petty larceny, auto theft, vandalism, and disorderly conduct were a few of the crimes that nearly cost DayMarr a basketball career.

After his most recent Tall Trees visit ruined his junior season, DayMarr decided to commit himself to basketball and not the streets. As a senior, he emerged as one of the best players in the city and committed to the University of Portland, where he knew no one and—secretly hoped—that the distance from Memphis would keep him safe and out of trouble.

DayMarr was a "gunner." He had a lightning-quick release and endless range. His confidence more than made up for his shot selection. DayMarr never met a shot he didn't like. Besides DayMarr, Manassas was pretty thin, but his nearly 30 points-per-game average managed to keep them competitive. He had done for Manassas what Memphis legend, Randy Culpepper, did for Sheffield back in the day. With only a few games left in the season, their hope of a playoff bid started with a win over MLK.

Both Stephon and DayMarr were two of the best in the city. Buzz on social media increased excitement around the game. Students at both high schools argued on X over who was the better player.

In the locker room, Lenny stood before the team, hands clasped behind his back. The players sat dejected, sipping Gatorade and grumbling. They were down by ten at halftime and hadn't scored any points in the last few minutes of the first half. Tim paced, his arms folded across his chest.

"We're better than them! Way better than them," Tim shouted.

Lenny nodded in agreement. "Manassas looks like they want it more. They're hungry."

"State is on the line," Tim shouted again before punching a locker with his fist. The players looked at Tim.

"Coach wants it. How about y'all?" Lenny asked, glaring at Stephon. "We win tonight, we're going down state. It's now or never."

"Sack up time!" Tim shouted again, still pacing.

"Make your own destiny," Lenny challenged. "Or someone else will make it for you. Bring it in."

The team gathered in a circle around Lenny. "I am the master of my fate," he bellowed.

"I am the captain of my soul," the team responded.

Manassas' home game crowds were historically hostile, and this one lived up to the reputation. Curse words and insults filled the gym. The hostility of the crowd reflected the animosity between the two schools, neighborhood conflicts, gang wars, and neighbors whose community had been neglected. Armed security guards stood at the entrance to each game.

Stephon opened the second half like a man possessed, his first three shots finding nothing but net to ignite a 6-0 MLK surge. The message was clear: he hadn't come this far to fold now.

What followed was pure theater—a heavyweight bout fought with basketball instead of fists. Stephon versus DayMarr, bucket for bucket, pride for pride. DayMarr had home court advantage and he milked every ounce, feeding off the crowd like a vampire. Each made shot sent him into his routine: chest puffed, arms spread wide, backpedaling down court while bellowing at the rafters like he owned the building.

But Stephon had ice in his veins. He matched DayMarr shot for shot, taunt for taunt, never giving an inch. The crowd tried to rattle him, but when he picked off a careless pass and exploded down court, even the hostile fans couldn't help themselves. The tomahawk dunk he threw down was so vicious it drew reluctant gasps from enemy territory.

Two alpha dogs circling each other, neither willing to blink first. The scoreboard was just keeping count—this was about something deeper than points.

At the end of the third quarter, MLK had cut Manassas' lead to two. Both Stephon and DayMarr had scored 25 points each.

The tension was high as the fourth quarter began. Before the referee blew the whistle, Tavon grabbed Stephon's jersey and pulled him close until they were face-to-face. With a smile, he smirked, "Bust his ass." Stephon smiled back and nodded in acknowledgment.

On the first possession of the fourth quarter, Stephon brought the ball down the right side of the lane and pulled up for a short jumper. Swish.

After a missed shot by Manassas on the other end, DaRon swept up the rebound and threw an outlet pass to Tavon, who started a break. He found Stephon on the left wing. Stephon went baseline, spun, switched hands, and threw down a one-handed dunk. DayMarr quickly answered, blowing by Terrance for a layup.

The rest of the fourth quarter was a seesaw game. Both teams exchanged baskets. The Stephon vs. DayMarr matchup had lived up to the hype. With a minute remaining, Stephon had scored 36 points to DayMarr's 35. MLK led by two points.

DayMarr brought the ball upcourt for Manassas. Just after he crossed midcourt, he calmly drained a three-pointer, catching Tavon with his hands down. The crowd erupted. Manassas led by one, 61-60.

Tavon brought the ball up the court for MLK. At midcourt, he easily broke Manassas' halfcourt press and zipped a chest pass to Terrance at the top of the key. Terrance's pump fake caused his defender to jump as he penetrated the paint. When the defense collapsed, Terrance bounced passed to Lenny, who snuck behind the defense for an easy clean dunk. Perfect, crisp ball movement.

The buzzer sounded. Game over. MLK 62, Manassas 61. Lenny hung his head and held back tears. MLK was going to the state tournament.

CHAPTER 45

Gaining a Father

In his office, Lenny watched edited game footage of Frayser High School on his laptop. Stats compiled the footage from YouTube clips on the school's page. Highlights were synced to Chris Travis' "Crunch Time." MLK didn't have the staff or resources to film their opponents' games, so Lenny and Tim relied on what Stats could unearth from the internet and word of mouth.

Most of Frayser's highlights featured senior River Parks. Lenny knew stopping him was the key to MLK's success in the state tournament.

Suddenly, while Lenny watched the film, there was a knock at the door. Lenny kept his attention on the screen but responded, "Come in." Eddie stuck his head in, and his eyes darted around the office. "Eddie, what's up, man?" Lenny greeted him with surprise.

"I was just in the neighborhood, so I figured I'd drop in," Eddie explained. He entered the room further and held up a bag from Wing Guru. "Hungry?"

Lenny nodded with a smile. "I am now."

"I figured you would be," Eddie agreed. He began unloading the bags of food. Then he stopped. "Your mother means a lot to me, Lenny."

Lenny paused the video and looked up from the screen. "I know. Everything good?" Lenny asked.

Eddie gushed, "A whole lot. I never thought I'd meet another woman. Or fall in love with another woman. I ain't the most spiritual man, but God has blessed me. He put your mother in my life. I believe that." Eddie took a seat opposite Lenny.

"What's up, Eddie?" Lenny's heart started to beat faster.

"I want to marry your mother. And I want to ask your permission. You're her only family."

Lenny's eyes widened. He sat back in his chair, rubbing his chin. He stammered, "Wow, marriage."

Eddie repeated, "Marriage."

"You're a good guy, Eddie, and I appreciate all you've done for me," Lenny said. "All I want is for my mom to be happy. You make her happy. You have my permission." Lenny extended his hand for Eddie to shake. "Welcome to the family."

Eddie shook Lenny's hand and then pulled him close for a bear hug, which startled Lenny. After the embrace, they both sat down. Eddie held up his hand, which was slightly shaking. Eddie breathed a sigh of relief. "Phew, I was nervous."

Lenny's shoulders slumped, and the smile faded from his face. "It's hard not to feel like I'm losing my mother," he confessed.

Eddie nodded and offered, "You're not losing your mother. You're gaining a father."

Lenny sat up and nodded his head in affirmation. "Thanks, Eddie. When are you going to ask her?"

"Tonight," Eddie proclaimed with confidence.

CHAPTER 46

Rivals - First Half

MURFREESBORO has served as home to the Tennessee state
finals for decades. For many players, Middle Tennessee State
University represents their first and final opportunity to play
competitively on a Division 1 court. For some, it symbolizes their
final official competitive game ever.

The university's coliseum held 11,500 seats. Only a few empty
chairs remained with five minutes left before tip-off in the first-
round matchup between Frayser and MLK. MLK fans donning gold
and black filled one side of the arena while Frayser's fans in red and
white blanketed the other. A four-hour drive would not prevent fans
from watching their team's final games. Don Trip and Starlito's
"Hoop Dreams" piped through the stadium speakers.

Lenny stood on the sidelines with his arms folded across his
chest and watched his team go through its pre-game warm-up. He
gazed around the arena. Being back at MTSU triggered a rush of
memories—his state championship run with Coach Heard. He
recalled the pride he felt as he held up the winner's trophy at center
court with his teammates.

Tim sidled up next to Lenny and nudged him with his elbow.
"Brings back a lot of memories, doesn't it?" Lenny nodded and
cracked a half-smile.

Tim turned around and scanned the MLK crowd. "I haven't seen this many folks turn out for a game in years. These kids will never forget this moment."

Lenny turned to scan the crowd, and his chest tightened with something he hadn't felt in years—people had actually shown up for him. There in the front row sat Principal Davenport flanked by Patricia and Eddie, all three beaming like proud parents. Their synchronized wave hit him like a warm embrace. He touched his forehead in a mock salute, grinning despite himself.

A few rows back, Stanley raised his Starbucks cup in a toast, the unmistakable glint in his eye confirming it wasn't coffee fueling his enthusiasm tonight. The old man winked and tilted his cup skyward—a gesture that said *here's to second chances* louder than any words could.

Lenny's smile widened as his gaze swept higher into the coliseum. Near the upper section, Cliff Bell and Zo were still hunting for seats, craning their necks like tourists in their own city. Even they'd made the trip.

For the first time in longer than he could remember, Lenny felt like he belonged somewhere. These weren't just spectators—they were his people, his unlikely family, all gathered to watch him try to piece his life back together one game at a time.

"You ready for this, Mr. MLK?" Jamel, who was seated in the makeshift VIP section behind MLK's bench, poked Lenny and asked.

"We're about to find out," Lenny replied.

Lenny wasn't the only one surveying the crowd. On the court, Stephon caught a pass in the layup line and threw it down with authority, but his eyes weren't on the rim—they were scanning the bleachers like a searchlight.

There. Not far from MLK's bench, his sisters had claimed their territory. Laila bounced in her seat, waving a poster that screamed "GO STEPHON" in bold letters that could be seen from space. Beside her, Tammy wrestled with her two boys, who treated the bleachers like their personal playground, climbing and squirming despite her best efforts to contain them.

The sight hit Stephon harder than he expected. His family. His people. Here for him when it mattered most.

He jogged to the other end, scooped a rebound, and fired a pass to Tavon for a layup, but his mind was elsewhere. As the ball swished through, Stephon's gaze drifted back to the stands, eyes searching, hoping, straining to pick out one more face in the sea of supporters.

Someone who should be there. Someone who would never be there again.

His chest tightened as he kept looking anyway, unable to stop himself from hoping for the impossible.

Stephon locked eyes with Sadat, and the two exchanged smiles.

"Aye, see all those college coaches sitting up front?" Tavon bellowed excitedly as he brushed past Terrence and Stephon in line. "No cap, we all might get signed tonight."

A wall of men in khakis and polo shirts with their school's logos lined the sidelines. Aside from all-star games, this was the final opportunity for players to make an impression on college coaches.

The horn sounded, and both teams ran to the bench. Stats wheeled out onto the court with Lenny and Tim close by to greet the team for the tip-off speech.

"Fellas, I want you to look out into the crowd at all the people from your community that you brought together," Lenny motioned towards the crowd. "That's who you're representing today. Not just yourselves, or me, or even that MLK on your shirt. You represent an entire community of people." Each player stared intently into Lenny's eyes, soaking up every word.

"Today, I want you to play your hearts out not only for us but for them."

"Yes, coach!" the team yelled in unison.

"Win on three," Stats announced with his fist held in the air. "One. Two. Three!"

"WIN!"

Tavon, Stephon, Harrison, Terrence, and DaRon strolled onto the court. Frayser's Frank Thomas, Ray Ray, and River Parks all migrated towards center court with revenge written on each of their faces.

From the tip-off, MLK dominated the first quarter. Using man-to-man defense, they stifled Frayser, allowing few opportunities for open threes. Frank Thomas struggled to get open as Stephon chased closely behind him on each screen, preventing him from creating space to shoot. When Frank was able to break free off a screen, he found another MLK teammate double-teaming him, forcing the pass.

DaRon and Terrence neutralized River Parks by fronting him in the post and bullying him near the basket. The big man struggled to get touches and picked up two frustration fouls that sent him to the bench near the middle of the quarter. Without River Parks to protect the basket, Stephon flourished in the paint.

"Stephon, post up!" yelled Lenny.

Tavon waved DaRon out of the post, and Stephon ran towards the strong side. Tavon lobbed an entry pass into Stephon, who made a quick spin around Frank Thomas and finished with an and-one at the rim.

First quarter: 19 - 10, MLK.

During a timeout, Lenny addressed the players in the huddle. "fellahs, great quarter. Remember, this team is scrappy. Don't let up. DaRon, stay aggressive in the post. No second-chance rebounds for them. Tavon, take your time on offense; we're up."

"Stephon, if they keep Frank on you, kill him," Tim added. "He can't guard you."

Stephon nodded his sweat-drenched head in agreement. Tavon slapped him on the back. "We got this, bruh." He peered over Stephon's shoulder at the college coaches sharing notes.

River Parks reentered the game in the second quarter despite having two fouls. Frayser changed its strategy. They switched to a 2-3 zone to protect Parks and neutralize Stephon's post attacks.

"Tavon, run overload," Lenny instructed from the sidelines.

Tavon slowly dribbled the ball up the sideline within arm's reach of every Division 1 college coach in the Midsouth. Instead of following the play call, he called his own number and shot a deep three-pointer from the key that barely grazed the rim.

Parks grabbed the rebound and launched an outlet pass to a streaking Ray Ray. Ray Ray caught the ball in stride and threw down a ferocious dunk over Terrence that caused Frayser fans to jump out of their seats. 19-12, MLK.

Stephon looked over towards Lenny as he trotted back on offense. He expected to see someone headed to the bench to replace Tavon, but he didn't. Lenny stood calmly on the sideline, clapping for his team.

"Tavon is out there hawking, coach; we need to pull him," Tim implored.

"I agree," Stats chimed in.

Lenny ignored them.

On the next play, Tavon dribbled the ball up the court and forced a lob pass intended for DaRon, but River Parks saw it coming and deflected the ball. Ray Ray picked up the loose ball and darted towards the rim again. This time Stephon met him and looked poised to block his shot, but Ray Ray completed a mid-air pass to Frank Thomas waiting open in the corner for a three-pointer, swish! 19-15 Frayser.

"Tavon, run the damn play," warned DaRon as he inbounded the ball.

Stephon looked at Lenny again and stared, confused.

Tavon brought the ball up the court again, dribbling timidly as his confidence began to fade. He attempted to run the play, which called for Stephon to run the baseline for a short corner pass from the wing. Harrison clapped to receive the pass on the wing, but Tavon threw it too late, and Frank intercepted it. Frank passed up a wide-open layup for a pull-up three. As the ball spiraled through the air, the Frayser crowd anticipated its destination, yelling together, "yoooooooooooooop" as the shot fell through the basket. 19-18, MLK.

Frustrated with Tavon's turnovers, Stephon clapped for Terrence to pass him the ball to run point. Stephon received the ball, waved off Tavon, and pushed past Frank Thomas with a hesitation dribble. Another Frayser defender attempted to double-team Stephon near the three-point line, but he split the trap, took one dribble, and exploded in the air for a towering finger roll above the rim.

"You gotta pull Tavon, coach. Let Stephon run the point," Tim advised.

"Run Memphis!" Lenny yelled at his team.

Immediately, MLK formed a half-court 1-3-1 trap, a defense that forced guards into the sidelines and often resulted in turnovers.

Ray Ray recognized the defense at half court and backed up before crossing. Then he flung a one-handed baseball pass to Frank Thomas, who stood wide open in the corner. When Lenny and Harrison converged on him for a trap, Frank tossed a lob pass to an open River Parks for a dunk. Foul. Parks swished the free throw. 21-21.

The two teams traded baskets all quarter, neither able to land a knockout blow. With ten seconds left and the score knotted at 30, Tavon gripped the ball at half-court, the weight of the final possession heavy in his hands.

The crowd noise faded to a dull roar as he surveyed the defense. Five seconds. Four. Stephon came flying up from the baseline, setting a bone-jarring screen that freed Tavon for his drive. The lane opened like a door to destiny.

But Frayser had seen this movie before. Two defenders converged on Tavon like heat-seeking missiles, trapping him in no-man's land. His dribble died in his hands as bodies pressed in from all sides, suffocating any hope of a clean look.

The buzzer's wail cut through the gym as Tavon stood frozen, ball clutched uselessly against his chest. College coaches all taking notes. The half ended with a whimper instead of the bang they'd scripted.

Both teams jogged toward their locker rooms, the scoreboard reading 30-30, but the real score was opportunity lost. In a game where every possession mattered, they wouldn't get another one.

CHAPTER 47

Rivals - Second Half

Part II

During halftime, the players sat in their wooden cubby holes inside MTSU's men's locker room. Lenny and Tim were still outside the locker discussing the first half. Inside, the players were having their own discussion.

"Tavon, pass the fucking ball, bruh," demanded Terrence.

"Nigga, for what? You got three points," Tavon shouted in response.

"I'd have more if it wasn't for your hawking ass."

"Shut up, and sit down," Lenny interjected as he and Tim entered the locker room.

The room fell silent as the players focused on Lenny pacing back and forth for fifteen seconds before finally speaking.

"Fifteen years ago, I was sitting right where you're sitting now. Coach Heard, one of the best coaches to ever do it, was standing where I am right now."

Tim looked Lenny in the eyes.

"We were down ten at the half to Northside. Seemed like every coach in the country was in the stands."

Tim shook his head in agreement.

"Coach told us, forget the bright lights, ignore the college coaches, block out the fans. The only thing that matters is the teammate sitting right next to you. Don't let that man down." Lenny pointed. "Don't let the team down."

"Yes, coach," the team responded in unison.

"Everything you need to win this game, you already know. It's up to you now. It's not on us."

"Yes, coach."

Tavon and Stephon glanced at each other.

"Everybody in the middle," Tim ordered.

"Warriors on three. One. Two. Three," added Stats.

"Warriors!"

Everyone sprinted out of the locker room except Tavon and Stephon. The two lingered behind and walked slowly beside each other.

"My bad, man. I know I'm playing like trash. But I need that scholarship. I may never get another chance like this," Tavon admitted.

"Any coach who doesn't recognize your skills is a fool. You're the best point guard in the city," Stephon replied. "That's on my pops."

Stephon embraced Tavon around the neck as they passed by Tim and Lenny, who overheard their conversation while standing in the doorway.

"Everyone has their own mountain to climb," Lenny noted proudly under his breath.

In the third quarter, Tavon and Stephon began working their magic. Stephon ran the point while Tavon played off the ball. Ray Ray struggled to keep up with Tavon's off-ball movement and found himself navigating a labyrinth of screens. Stephon showcased his passing abilities, finding Tavon open on fade picks and backdoor cuts for buckets. On five consecutive possessions, Tavon either scored or got fouled.

Halfway into the third quarter, Frayser called a timeout as the game began to slip away.

"Fellas, we're up twelve points. One possession at a time. Keep playing like we're behind," Lenny pleaded.

As Lenny continued his speech, Stephon nudged Tavon in the huddle to look up at the scoreboard. The jumbotron displayed Tavon's highlights. Tavon looked back at Stephon, and the two smiled.

"Don't let up!" Lenny yelled as Tavon, Stephon, DaRon, Terrence, and Harrison headed back onto the court.

Two minutes left in the third, MLK nursing a comfortable 47-35 cushion that felt anything but safe. Ray Ray pushed the tempo coming out of the timeout, whipping a crisp pass to Frank Thomas on the wing. Frank caught and looked inside, trying to thread an entry pass to River Parks in the paint.

DaRon had other plans. He slipped around Parks like smoke through pursed lips, fingertips deflecting the pass into Stephon's waiting hands. Stephon's eyes flashed up court where Tavon was already in full flight, a blur racing toward an easy score.

The pass was perfect. Tavon gathered it in stride, legs coiling for takeoff as Parks desperately sprinted back to contest. What happened next unfolded in horrifying slow motion.

Tavon launched himself skyward just as Parks slid underneath him—not maliciously, just mistimed. Physics took over. Tavon's legs caught Parks' shoulder, sending him into a violent somersault, arms flailing helplessly, the ball floating in space, as gravity betrayed him.

The landing came hard and wrong. A sickening *thud* echoed through the coliseum like a gunshot, followed by the collective gasp of eleven thousand people who'd just witnessed something that shouldn't happen to anyone.

Silence. Then the scramble of coaches and trainers rushing onto the court.

MLK players rushed to Tavon's side as he grimaced from the pain. DaRon extended his hand, encouraging his injured teammate to shake off the pain.

"Don't move him!" Lenny screamed as he rushed out onto the floor with an on-site trainer to attend to Tavon.

Stephon, DaRon, Terrence, and Harrison huddled together near half court with their heads down in deep thought. MLK's bench interlocked their arms and bowed their heads in prayer.

Moments later, two trainers pushed a squeaky-wheeled stretcher onto the court. The two lifted Tavon off the ground and placed him on the gurney. Tavon lay still on the gurney with his eyes open, staring at the ceiling as the two trainers pushed him towards the locker room tunnel. Principal Davenport and Lenny escorted Tavon to the locker room.

"Everybody to the sideline!" Tim yelled as he waved over to his team. "Stephon, you stay and shoot the free throws for Tavon. DJ, go in for Tavon."

Stephon knocked in both free throws to end the third quarter.

The final quarter of the state championship quarterfinals began. Lenny and Tavon remained in the locker room, while MLK led the game 49-35. In the huddle, Tim did his best to keep his team focused on the game.

"We have eight more minutes of basketball left. Tavon would have wanted us to finish this out strong. He's a warrior; he's going to be fine."

DaRon and Terrence nodded in agreement.

"Go out there and win this!" Tim shouted.

Frayser smelled blood. Stephon dribbled the ball up the court and was met with an unexpected trap. He picked up his dribble and attempted to call a timeout, but Frank Thomas poked the ball out of his hands and went the other way for an easy layup. 49-37 MLK.

DaRon inbounded the ball to Stephon again. This time he beat the trap with a one-two crossover up the sideline. He tossed the ball to DJ—an inexperienced freshman who moved up to varsity halfway through the season—and he fumbled the pass out of bounds. Frayser's Ray Ray quickly inbounded the ball to River Parks and got it right back. He zipped up the court and found an open Frank Thomas on the wing. Thomas pump-faked and got Terrence in the air before launching a step-back three-pointer that banked in. 49-40 MLK.

"I think we need a timeout, coach," Stats warned Tim.

"Let them play through it," Tim replied as he eyed the tunnel, searching for Lenny.

Stephon pushed the ball up the court again and called for a screen from DaRon at the top of the key. He navigated the screen with a quick in-and-out dribble that froze DaRon's defender as he blew past him. Stephon took two dribbles toward the rim and elevated for a vicious dunk. The whistle blew as DaRon high-fived Stephon.

"Charge!" yelled a referee as he put his right hand behind his head and pointed the other way with his left.

"What?! Come on, ref, that's bullshit!" exclaimed Tim.

Another whistle blew.

"Technical foul. MLK's bench."

"What?!" yelled Tim as he jumped up and down.

"Calm down, coach," pleaded Stats. "You're the only coach we have left."

Tim held in his anger and sat down in his chair, fuming.

Frank Thomas made both free throws, and Frayser maintained possession. From the sideline, Frank Thomas made an entry pass to River Parks in the post, who had DaRon sealed. The big man took one drop step and overpowered DaRon, bullying him under the basket and making a layup. 49-44 MLK. Two minutes left in the game.

Tim held his head in his hands. He felt a pat on his back.

"What, Stats?" Tim grumbled.

"Scoot over," Lenny instructed.

"Lenny! What happened? How's Tavon?" Tim queried.

"He's going to be fine. Might be a deep bruise in his knee."

"Thank God, man."

Lenny stood up from his chair and motioned to the referee. "Timeout, ref."

The team noticed Lenny and rushed to the sideline.

"Coach, what's up with Tavon?" asked Stephon.

"Yeah, is he good?" DaRon chimed in.

"Tavon is fine. He's not coming back, but he'll live."

The players all appeared relieved.

"Now, we've got some business to take care of. We have two minutes left in this game. Protect the ball and stay aggressive."

Stephon, DaRon, Terrence, DJ, and Harrison reentered the game. Stephon brought the ball up the court and noticed that Frayser had fallen back into a two-three zone. The move confused Lenny, who motioned to Stephon to run short corner.

"Coach, they're running zone because our only shooter and ball handler is Stephon," Stats remarked.

Lenny immediately understood the strategy. Stephon passed the ball to DJ on the wing, who zipped a pass to Harrison in the short corner. Harrison pulled up for a jumper and missed badly. River Parks recovered the ball and sent an overhead pass to a streaking

Frank Thomas. Instead of converting the layup, Frank pulled the ball back out behind the three-point line and hoisted a high-arching three into the air. The ball seemed to rotate through the coliseum forever. A whistle blew. The ball fell into the net. DaRon was called for the foul.

Forty-five seconds remained in the game as Frank Thomas stepped to the free throw line and knocked down the extra point. 49-48 MLK.

With no shot clock to worry about, Lenny signaled to his team to spread the court and run out the clock with Stephon handling the ball. Lenny knew that Frank Thomas could not stop Stephon one-on-one, and if they doubled, Stephon would make the right pass.

Stephon crossed half-court with thirty-two seconds separating MLK from victory. He hugged the ball close, dribbling low and tight while Frank shadowed his every move. The entire coliseum had risen as one, eleven thousand voices creating a wall of sound that seemed to bend time itself.

Twenty seconds. Fifteen. Ten.

Frayser's coach frantically signaled from the sideline — foul him, foul him now. Frank lunged forward, his hand slapping down across Stephon's forearm. The ball squirted loose as Stephon stumbled, waiting for the whistle that never came.

Frank couldn't believe his luck. He scooped up the loose ball and exploded toward the other end with Stephon in desperate pursuit. Five seconds. Four. The crowd's roar turned to horror as Frank took three hard dribbles and launched himself toward the rim.

Time suspended. Frank rose with the ball cocked for what felt like the easiest layup of his life. The glass waited above him, victory just a soft touch away.

Then Stephon arrived like thunder. His hand met ball against backboard with a *crack* that silenced the building—a rejection so perfect it defied physics. The MLK faithful erupted in pure ecstasy.

But the celebration died as a whistle's shrill cry cut through the chaos. Every eye in the coliseum turned to the referee.

The clock read 0.0 seconds. Everything hung in the balance.

"Goaltending!" a referee called as he rotated his index finger in the air in a circular motion.

Uproars from both fan bases erupted.

Ball game.

50-49 Frayser.

CHAPTER 48

We Gone Be Alright

The next day, Stephon lay in his bed blasting Kendrick Lamar's "Alright" through AirPods. He kept rewinding the chorus, reciting the words. He was still recovering, mentally and physically, from Saturday's state championship loss. Both his legs and ankles were wrapped with ice packs. He scrolled through Instagram and came across a photo from Tavon's page. In the pic, Tavon sat up in a hospital bed, flexing with his leg wrapped in a cast. The photo's caption read:

Pain is temporary. #rehabszn

Seeing Tavon in good spirits made Stephon smile. He dropped a comment under the photo with a gorilla emoji:

Big facts, bro.

As he continued to scroll through Instagram, he received a notification from Sadat.

[MLKfinest has entered the chat room and game]

Sadat: Great game yesterday. You guys played your hearts out.

MLKfinest: Yeah, tough loss. Thanks for coming all the way down to see us play.

Sadat: Of course. I got some good news.

MLKfinest: What's up?

Sadat: This is our last session.

MLKfinest: How's that good news?

Sadat: I'm moving back to ATL to be closer to my son. I reached out to him for the first time in years, and he wants me to watch his matches.

MLKfinest: That's what's up.

Sadat: I have you to thank for it.

MLKfinest: Me?

Sadat: Watching you play yesterday made me realize what I'm missing.

MLKfinest: Bet that.

Sadat: That's only part of the good news.

MLKfinest: Forreal?

Sadat: This is also our last session because the prosecutor in your case isn't going to pursue charges against you anymore.

MLKfinest: You lying.

Sadat: I spoke with the DA. We're old friends. I helped his daughter through a drug addiction. I walked him through your file, and he promised the prosecutor in your case would let it go.

MLKfinest: Thank you, Sadat!!! [100% emoji] So, this was your goal all along?

Sadat: [wink emoji] The game is chess, Steph. Always remember that . . . now, how about one last game? Your move.

MLKFinest: [white pawn E2 to E4]

CHAPTER 49

New Beginnings

Jamel carried a large moving box from the house, struggling under its weight. When he reached the back of the U-Haul truck, he clumsily set it on the ground, nearly dropping the box. He rested his palms on his knees, closed his eyes, and took a deep breath. "Man, this box is heavy as hell."

Lenny chuckled as he hopped down from the back of the truck. "You're just out of shape." Inside the U-Haul were neatly stacked moving boxes.

Jamel waved him off. "I'm in great shape. Tip-top shape."

They both laughed. Patricia emerged from the house, carrying a pitcher of iced tea and two mason jar glasses. A modest gold engagement ring was noticeably on her left ring finger.

Jamel's eyes perked up. "Your famous sweet tea?" Patricia nodded. "That's what I'm talking about, Aunt P!" Jamel moved toward Patricia, hands out. Patricia smiled, poured Jamel's glass full, and handed it to him. He eagerly drained the glass and raised it for a refill. "Best tea in Memphis," Jamel praised.

Lenny wiped his hands on his pants and walked over. Patricia filled the second glass with sweet tea and handed it to Lenny.

"Thanks, Ma."

Patricia smiled. "You're welcome."

"I'm starving," Jamel moaned.

Patricia, bemused, shook her head. "Dinner is almost done."

Jamel perked up again. "What are you cooking?"

"Grilled salmon with roasted fennel and tomatoes. Eddie is making a treacle tart for dessert."

Jamel responded with a blank look. "Aunt P, I don't know what any of that is, but beggars can't be choosers."

Patricia chuckled. "You won't be disappointed."

"Also, let me know if you want me to perform at your wedding. I can make that happen."

Patricia and Lenny both laughed. "Eddie and I are not having a wedding," Patricia replied. "We're having a civil ceremony at the courthouse."

"Well, if you change your mind, let me know," Jamel offered.

"I will."

Principal Davenport's red Mercedes pulled into the driveway.

"What's Trina doing here?" Lenny asked aloud.

"I invited her," Patricia conceded. She turned to Jamel. "Help me inside."

Jamel snickered. "Fa sho." He nudged Lenny in the ribs.

Jamel and Patricia walked back into the house. Lenny met Principal Davenport at her car as she stepped out of the driver's side. Lenny greeted her with a "Hey."

"Hey you," Principal Davenport replied. "Your mom invited me. Your farewell dinner."

Lenny smiled. "I'm just moving down the street."

"New beginnings are always good."

Lenny nodded in agreement.

After dinner, Lenny walked Principal Davenport to her car. Night had fallen, and the newly installed pathway lights illuminated the driveway.

"I'm stuffed," Principal Davenport moaned, rubbing her stomach. "Your mom's cooking is exquisite, and Eddie's tart was incredible."

"They're a match made in culinary heaven," Lenny quipped.

Principal Davenport approved. "I'm happy for them. It's nice to find someone to share your time and hobbies with. To grow old with. I thought I had that when I got married. Thought wrong."

Lenny shrugged. "You can still have that." They reached the driver's side door of Principal Davenport's car. Lenny cleared his throat. "This was fun. Eating dinner together. We should do it again. For real. At a restaurant."

Principal Davenport grinned. "Are you asking me out on a date?"

Lenny blushed. "Yes, I am."

Principal Davenport smiled. "I'd like that." She slid into the driver's seat. "Oh, I almost forgot." She plucked a sealed envelope from the passenger seat and handed it to Lenny.

"You wrote me a letter?" Lenny asked.

Principal Davenport smirked and shook her head no. "It's an official contract renewal letter to remain the head boy's basketball coach at Martin Luther King High School. Welcome back, Lenny."

Lenny grinned widely. He held the letter with both hands. "Wow."

Principal Davenport returned the smile. "Congrats, Lenny. You deserve it."

CHAPTER 50

A Better Tomorrow

Peter Haskins, a burly white man with curly gray hair in a navy blazer, sat across from Lenny's desk, eating a Boston cream donut. He dusted the crumbs from his lapels.

Peter covered high school sports, particularly high school basketball, for The Commercial Appeal. He had been covering it for almost forty years and possessed an encyclopedic knowledge of Memphis high school basketball. He wrote a biography of Memphis great Larry Finch in the early 1990s that raised his national profile, but he turned down offers from bigger newspapers to remain in his hometown, Memphis.

Peter was an honest journalist, and his love for basketball was genuine. He and Coach Heard would talk basketball for hours, two basketball historians exchanging stories and comparing their favorite players. Peter became a fixture at MLK games when Coach Heard was coaching. He wrote a feature on Lenny when he was a high school senior and another piece when Lenny was trying his hand at the NBA.

Lenny entered his office with Tim in tow. "Mr. Haskins," Lenny said, extending his hand. The two shook hands warmly. "Remember Tim?"

"I do," Peter replied, nodding in Tim's direction.

Lenny took his seat behind his desk, and Tim sat in an office chair in the corner.

"Fellas, I appreciate your time," Peter said. "Man, it feels like old times here. Coach Heard and I had a whole mess of conversations in this office. He was one of a kind."

"Absolutely," Lenny agreed.

"Miss the big fella," Tim said wistfully.

Peter sat up, pulled a tape recorder from his jacket pocket, and clicked it on. "No use in talking about the past. I'm here to discuss the future and the resurgence of MLK. Hell of a season, coach. It surprised me to see you back home and able to get these boys back to the playoffs. You did a yeoman's job. Hats off to you."

Lenny smiled with appreciation. "Thanks, Mr. Haskins. MLK is home. While I was initially hesitant to take over, I owed it to MLK and Coach Heard. People say I saved the team, but really, the team saved me. Coming home was the best decision I've made in years."

Peter nodded and rubbed his chin. "Stephon re-emerged after some issues and led the team. I've seen him play. He's the real deal. Next season, he's got to be there every game for this team to win State. How do you keep him on the straight and narrow?"

"Stephon, like many ballplayers in Memphis, comes from a tough background," Lenny responded. "But he's put those issues behind him. He's ready. He'll be training and playing ball all summer, getting ready for the upcoming season." Lenny paused. "Stephon is the best player in Memphis, and I believe he's one of the best players in the country. He's going to prove that next season. For Stephon and MLK, there's only a better tomorrow."

CHAPTER 51

Brothers

Sunnybrook was quiet, even for a Sunday night, with only a handful of customers. A middle-aged black couple two-stepped near the jukebox to Bobby "Blue" Bland's "I Pity the Fool."

Lenny sat at the bar across from Cliff, drinking a glass of ice water while hovering over a steaming plate of sauce-dripping hot wings and fries.

"I got something for you." Cliff reached into his inner jacket pocket and removed a vintage Polaroid of Lenny and Zo's AAU 13-under championship photo. In the photo, the team surrounded Lenny and Zo, holding up the trophy together, with Cliff standing by their side.

Lenny rubbed the wing sauce from his hands on a napkin and took the photo. "Wow, this is a real throwback." He smiled as he reminisced.

"Yep, the good old days."

Bells tinkled as Sunnybrook's front door swung open, and Zo entered, wearing a colorful AMIRI sweatsuit and Jordan 1 lows. He sat down next to Lenny.

Zo nodded to Cliff. "What up, Pops?"

Cliff nodded back. "Good to see you, son. Been a while. I was wondering when you'd make it here."

Zo shrugged. "Just been busy. You been getting the money I sent?"

"Every month." Cliff nodded.

He turned to Lenny. "I'd offer you a drink, but I see you're nursing that water over there."

Lenny smirked but didn't speak.

"I saw your car at Shelby Farms the other day."

"Oh yea?" Lenny sounded aloof.

"Yea, me and Katrina . . ." Zo tried to explain.

"Don't even matter, bro." Lenny cut him off. "Have a seat man." Lenny clapped Zo's shoulder and pulled him close. Whatever happened at Shelby Farms was miles behind them now. Katrina was her own woman, he was his own man—and this here, this was brotherhood. Stronger than old mistakes.

"We celebrating your return home?" Cliff asked, trying to lighten the mood.

Zo exhaled deeply. "My retirement."

"What?!" Lenny exclaimed.

"You serious, son?" Cliff asked.

"It's been a good run, but my heart isn't in it anymore." Zo shrugged. "It's time to see what's next for me."

Cliff nodded, poured a shot of Louis XIII, and handed it to Zo.

Zo raised the shot and downed it. He turned to Lenny. "Saw you guys at the state championship game. That kid Stephon is special."

"Yeah, my guys played hard," Lenny responded. "Proud of 'em. Steph is special."

"For real, when I saw you out there coaching those boys, I realized that what you're doing is more meaningful than any game I've ever played in my entire career."

Lenny turned to Zo and then glanced at Cliff, who was watching them both. "That means a lot. For real."

The door opened, and a beautiful woman stood in the doorway with her arms folded, impatiently tapping her feet and checking her watch. All three looked over at her.

"Well. She ain't here for us," Cliff stated, turning his attention to Zo.

"Money and fame have their perks. I ain't gonna lie." Zo stood up from the bar. He held the AAU photo up close and took one last look before handing it back to Lenny. "But no amount of money can replace family."

He extended his hand. "Brothers?"

Lenny stood up, accepted the handshake, and the two embraced. "Brothers for life."

Zo then turned to Cliff and nodded his head. Cliff returned the nod.

As Zo walked out of Sunnybrook, the jukebox played Bobby Blue Bland's "This Time I'm Gone For Good."

CHAPTER 52

You Got Next

O n a cool gray afternoon, Lenny stood in front of Coach Heard's tombstone and said a silent prayer. He removed a Yoo-Hoo from the pocket of his hoodie and placed it atop the headstone.

Lenny chuckled to himself. "You won't believe it, but I started drinking these too. I see why you were hooked."

Lenny rocked back and forth gently. "I'm going to be back at MLK, coaching again next year. Life moves fast. But like you always said, 'direction, not speed'"

Lenny sat on the ground, his hands atop his knees. "Got this kid, Stephon, who's the real deal. You would like him. He reminds me a little of myself. I think we can win the championship next season. Bring it home to MLK again." Lenny smiled at the thought.

A few minutes passed before Lenny rose to his feet. He wiped off the back of his pants. "I'll never be the coach you were, but I hope I can make a difference. Hope I can make you proud." Lenny ran his hand along the length of the top of the tombstone. "I'll be back soon. Even in heaven, you can't get rid of me!"

LATER THAT AFTERNOON

With nightfall approaching, Stephon shot jumpers on a basketball court in Gooch Park. The park was empty except for him and a teenage couple making out on the picnic tables. He moved around the court, dribbling and then shooting.

Lenny leaned against the chain-link fence and watched. The asphalt had recently been repaved and looked much better than when Lenny played pickup games there years ago. Back in junior high and high school, Lenny and Zo would crisscross Memphis, looking for pickup games, testing themselves against older players. They would sometimes wait hours to play. Those pickup games were where you earned your stripes.

"Snap your wrist," Lenny barked. Startled, Stephon missed the jump shot and turned to Lenny. "Snap your wrist," Lenny repeated. He made his way onto the court and retrieved the missed shot. "When you release, snap your wrist."

"Ok Thomas Shephard," Stephon chuckled.

"You got jokes." Lenn smiled. "I shot 40% from downtown senior year," Lenny boasted. "Think you can hit 40% next season?" Lenny passed Stephon the ball.

"Say less," Stephon responded with gravitas.

Lenny chuckled. "I hear you talking. We'll see."

Stephon dribbled between his legs. "You really mean what you said in the newspaper? That I'm the best player in Memphis?" Stephon stopped dribbling.

Lenny nodded. "I do. But it's up to you. Leave the nonsense in the streets. Just basketball and books. Nothing else. Can you do that?"

"Yeah," Stephon said with a proud grin. "I want my name to mean something. The way the old dudes talk about you, I want that."

"Don't worry, you got next," Lenny assured him.

Stephon bounced the ball and passed it to Lenny. "One-on-one to eleven. Loser buys Chings."

Lenny laughed. "You really think you can beat me?" He pointed to his own chest.

"Come get this work, old man," Stephon boasted.

Lenny chuckled. "Bet, game on."

Epilogue

Tammy decided to return to school to become a licensed beautician. She has plans to open her own hair salon in Memphis.

Laila graduated magna cum laude from Spelman College with a degree in psychology. She is currently working in Atlanta as a schoolteacher. She started a non-profit for teenage girls.

Zo Bell announced his retirement after 12 years in the league. He finally settled down, found a wife, and they moved to Los Angeles. His son, Cliff Bell Jr., was born shortly after they relocated.

Cliff Bell continues to run Sunnybrook. After Zo was traded, the two started a ritual of talking once a week to catch up on lost time. Cliff plans to visit California to see his grandson for the first time.

Stats finished his junior year at the top of his class. He was invited to a summer camp in Silicon Valley for gifted high school students. He plans to return next season as MLK's student assistant coach.

Tim accepted a job as an assistant principal at Carver High School. Tim and Lenny remain close. The two play in a 30-and-up basketball league at Gaston on weekends.

Principal Davenport was offered the superintendent position by the school board, but she declined. She continues to serve as principal at MLK. She and Lenny are dating again.

Tavon Graham received a full scholarship to the University of Memphis after his performance in the state championship. He scored high enough on the ACT to qualify for admission in the fall and will join the team next semester.

Harrison Fields, Terrence Price, and DaRon Scott all received scholarship offers from various schools. They all plan to return to MLK for next season.

Eddie and Patricia are happily married and moved to Florida to retire on the beach. They host holiday events at their home.

Sadat moved to Atlanta and became his son's biggest fan. He continues to mentor at-risk youth using the game of chess. He and Stephon remain close.

Stephon finished his junior year as the top player in the state of Tennessee. ESPN ranked him #20 at his position. Despite his run-in with the law, he received 20 full scholarship offers from Division I colleges. He plans to return to MLK for his senior year and take the team to the state championship.

Lenny was named Tennessee High School Coach of the Year. He visits Coach Heard's gravesite every week. He settled into his own place and now runs the AA meetings he used to attend. He finally let go of his dreams of making the NBA and dedicates his time to coaching and mentoring young boys who live in his old neighborhood. He and Stephon play chess together in their free time. He's happy to call Principal Davenport his girlfriend again.

Acknowledgements

Martinis M. Jackson

This book is for my first non-familial love—basketball—and for every athlete, fan, and soul whose life has been shaped by the game.

It's also a tribute to my hometown, Memphis, Tennessee—a city forged in pain and perseverance, with a cultural richness too often buried beneath narratives of despair.

The story was inspired by the countless young men my coauthor and I have encountered in our cities—kids who've carried the hopes of entire communities on their backs, all chasing the same dream: an NBA contract.

This book wouldn't exist without my coauthor, Manny Geraldo. Together, we chipped away at the stone for years until we carved out something worth sharing.

Thank you to those who pushed me forward, especially my wife, Molly, who never let me give up; my cousin, Kristina Watkis, who read early drafts and spoke positivity into existence; my brother, Tyres, who lifted me up when I felt like I had hit rock bottom; and LHW, a listening ear and critical eye when I needed it most.

Manny Geraldo II

This book has been years in the making, and I begin by giving thanks to God—for His grace, His guidance, and the strength to see this project through.

To the readers: thank you for opening this book, for giving our characters a home in your imagination, and for giving our words a chance. You make this journey worthwhile, and I hope the story resonates with you as much as it does with me.

Writing a book isn't easy. Sharing it with the world is even harder. What made this journey not only possible but also profoundly rewarding was the privilege of writing it alongside my close friend, Martinis Jackson. Thank you, Martinis, for your insight, your partnership, and your belief in this story. I'm grateful for every step we took together, and I'm already looking forward to our next collaboration.

To my wife, Lauren—thank you for your unwavering support, your honest and constructive feedback, and for always encouraging me to write.

And finally, for my daughters, Madison and Mackenzie—you are the light of my life. Every word I write is colored by the joy of being your dad. Thank you for reminding me of the magic in storytelling every single day. #GirlDad

APPENDIX A

MLK High School Basketball 2024–2025 Season Results

Game	Opponent	Score (MLK-Opp)	Leading Scorer
1	Cordova	46–76	Tavon Graham
2	Middle College	63–45	Tavon Graham
3	Frayser	67–66	Stephon Johnson
4	Oakhaven	58–51	DaRon Scott
5	Melrose	70–55	Tavon Graham
6	Kingsbury	64–60	Stephon Johnson
7	Hamilton	61–52	Terrence Price
8	MAHS	59–58	Stephon Johnson
9	Whitehaven	71–68	Tavon Graham
10	Fairley	66–61	Stephon Johnson
11	Hillcrest	62–57	DaRon Scott

12	Overton	69–62	Terrence Price
13	Craigmont	64–60	Tavon Graham
14	Trezevant	72–68	Stephon Johnson
15	Mitchell	70–67	Terrence Price
16	Raleigh-Egypt	65–59	DaRon Scott
17	Manassas	68–63	Stephon Johnson
18	Sheffield	63–61	Terrence Price
19	Kingsbury	66–64	Tavon Graham
20	Northside	76–75	Stephon Johnson
21	Melrose	60–55	Tavon Graham
22	Oakhaven	65–58	Stephon Johnson
23	Middle College	61–60	Terrence Price
24	Frayser	68–67	Stephon Johnson
25	Hamilton	70–66	DaRon Scott
26	City Championship	70-60	Tavon Graham
27	Overton	69–62	Tavon Graham
28	Craigmont	67–61	Terrence Price
29	Manassas	62–61	Stephon Johnson
30	State Championship Quarterfinals	49-50	Stephon Johnson

APPENDIX B

The Game Owes Me — Playlist

A curated playlist of the music featured throughout the book.

- **"Alright"** – Kendrick Lamar
- **"Choices"** – Project Pat
- **"Da Game Owes Me"** – Playa Fly
- **"Drunk By Myself"** – Nas
- **"Hoop Dreams"** – Don Trip and Starlito
- **"Honey Bee"** – Muddy Waters
- **"I Pity the Fool"** – Bobby "Blue" Bland
- **"Leave Some Day"** - Kevo Muney
- **"Let's Go"** – Key Glock
- **"Little Red Rooster"** – Howlin' Wolf
- **"Love Yourz"** – J. Cole
- **"Lovely Day"** – Bill Withers
- **"Me Against the World"** – 2Pac
- **"Me and You"** – Cassie
- **"Memphis Blues"** – W.C. Handy
- **"Nobody Needs Nobody"** – Playa Fly
- **"No More Pain"** – 2Pac

- **"Not Like Us"** – Kendrick Lamar

- **"Soul Man"** – Sam & Dave

- **"Tasty Love"** – Freddie Jackson

- **"This Time I'm Gone For Good"** – Bobby "Blue" Bland

- **"Time Today"** – Moneybagg Yo

- **"The World is Yours"** – Nas

- **"Walk Em Down"** – NLE Choppa

- **"What Kind of Woman is This"** – Buddy Guy

- **"Yeah Glo!"** – GloRilla

www.ingramcontent.com/pod-product-compliance
Lightning Source LLC
Chambersburg PA
CBHW020619110726
47899CB00002B/572